WAR AND PEACE
BOOK SIX : 1808-10

By Leo Tolstoy

War and Peace Book 6
by Leo Tolstoy

Copyright © 2025

All Rights reserved.
No part of this publication may be reproduced, stored in a retrieval system, or transmitted in any form or by any means, electronic, mechanical, photocopying or Otherwise, without the written permission of the publisher.

The author/editor asserts the moral right to be identified as the author/editor of this work.

ISBN: 978-93-94973-90-9

Published by
DOUBLE 9 BOOKS
2/13-B, Ansari Road
Daryaganj, New Delhi - 110002
info@double9books.com
www.double9books.com
Tel. 011-40042856

This book is under public domain

Printed in India.

About the Author

Leo Tolstoy was a Russian creator known for his books War and Peace which is viewed as the best book of pragmatist fiction. Tolstoy is additionally viewed as world's best author by quite a few people. Additionally an ethical scholar and a social reformer, Tolstoy had extreme moralistic points of view. In later life, he turned into an intense Christian rebel and anarcho-conservative.

Leo Tolstoy Born in Yasnaya Polyana on September 9, 1828, He had a place with a notable honorable Russian family. He was the fourth among five offspring of Count Nikolai Ilyich Tolstoy and Countess Mariya Tolstaya, both of whom kicked the bucket passing on their youngsters to be raised by family members.

In 1844, Tolstoy was acknowledged into Kazan University. Incapable to graduate past the subsequent year, Tolstoy got back to Yasnava Polyana and afterward invested energy going among Moscow and St. Petersburg. With some functioning information on a few dialects, he turned into a multilingual. Yet again the recently observed youth pulled in Tolstoy towards drinking, visiting massage parlors and most betting which left him in weighty obligation and anguish however Tolstoy before long acknowledged he was carrying on with a brutish life and endeavored college tests with the expectation that he would acquire a situation with the public authority, yet finished yet up in Caucuses serving in the military continuing in the strides of his senior sibling.

In Year 1862, Leo Tolstoy wedded Sophia Andreevna Behrs, generally called Sonya, who was 16 years more youthful than him. The couple had thirteen youngsters, of which, five passed on at an early age. Sonya went about as Tolstoy's secretary, editor and monetary chief while he made two out of his most prominent works. Their initial wedded life was loaded up with happiness.

He started composing his show-stopper, War and Peace in 1862. The six volumes of the work were distributed somewhere in the range of 1863 and 1869. With 580 characters got from history and others made by Tolstoy, this extraordinary novel takes on investigating the hypothesis of history and the irrelevance of noted figures like Alexander and Napoleon. Anna Karenina, Tolstoy's next epic was begun in 1873 and distributed totally in 1878.

Contents

BOOK SIX : 1808-10

CHAPTER I	7
CHAPTER II	10
CHAPTER III	13
CHAPTER IV	16
CHAPTER V	20
CHAPTER VI	26
CHAPTER VII	29
CHAPTER VIII	34
CHAPTER IX	37
CHAPTER X	40
CHAPTER XI	45
CHAPTER XII	49
CHAPTER XIII	52
CHAPTER XIV	56
CHAPTER XV	60
CHAPTER XVI	63
CHAPTER XVII	67
CHAPTER XVIII	70
CHAPTER XIX	75
CHAPTER XX	77
CHAPTER XXI	81
CHAPTER XXII	85
CHAPTER XXIII	89
CHAPTER XXIV	95
CHAPTER XXV	98
CHAPTER XXVI	102

BOOK SIX : 1808-10

CHAPTER I

Prince Andrew had spent two years continuously in the country.
All the plans Pierre had attempted on his estates—and constantly changing from one thing to another had never accomplished—were carried out by Prince Andrew without display and without perceptible difficulty.

He had in the highest degree a practical tenacity which Pierre lacked, and without fuss or strain on his part this set things going.

On one of his estates the three hundred serfs were liberated and became free agricultural laborers—this being one of the first examples of the kind in Russia. On other estates the serfs' compulsory labor was commuted for a quitrent. A trained midwife was engaged for Bogucharovo at his expense, and a priest was paid to teach reading and writing to the children of the peasants and household serfs.

Prince Andrew spent half his time at Bald Hills with his father and his son, who was still in the care of nurses. The other half he spent in "Bogucharovo Cloister," as his father called Prince Andrew's estate. Despite the indifference to the affairs of the world he had expressed to Pierre, he diligently followed all that went on, received many books, and to his surprise noticed that when he or his father had visitors from Petersburg, the very vortex of life, these people lagged behind himself—who never left the country—in knowledge of what was happening in home and foreign affairs.

Besides being occupied with his estates and reading a great variety of books, Prince Andrew was at this time busy with a critical survey of our last two unfortunate campaigns, and with drawing up a proposal for a reform of the army rules and regulations.

In the spring of 1809 he went to visit the Ryazán estates which had been inherited by his son, whose guardian he was.

Warmed by the spring sunshine he sat in the *calèche* looking at the new grass, the first leaves on the birches, and the first puffs of white spring clouds floating across the clear blue sky. He was not thinking of anything, but looked absent-mindedly and cheerfully from side to side.

They crossed the ferry where he had talked with Pierre the year before. They went through the muddy village, past threshing floors and green fields of winter rye, downhill where snow still lodged near the bridge, uphill where the clay had been liquefied by the rain, past strips of stubble land and bushes touched with green here and there, and into a birch forest growing on both sides of the road. In the forest it was almost hot, no wind could be felt. The birches with their sticky green leaves were motionless, and lilac-colored flowers and the first blades of green grass were pushing up and lifting last year's leaves. The coarse evergreen color of the small fir trees scattered here and there among the birches was an unpleasant reminder of winter. On entering the forest the horses began to snort and sweated visibly.

Peter the footman made some remark to the coachman; the latter assented. But apparently the coachman's sympathy was not enough for Peter, and he turned on the box toward his master.

"How pleasant it is, your excellency!" he said with a respectful smile.

"What?"

"It's pleasant, your excellency!"

"What is he talking about?" thought Prince Andrew. "Oh, the spring, I suppose," he thought as he turned round. "Yes, really everything is green already.... How early! The birches and cherry and alders too are coming out.... But the oaks show no sign yet. Ah, here is one oak!"

At the edge of the road stood an oak. Probably ten times the age of the birches that formed the forest, it was ten times as thick and twice as tall as they. It was an enormous tree, its girth twice as great as a man could embrace, and evidently long ago some of its branches had been broken off and its bark scarred. With its huge ungainly limbs sprawling unsymmetrically, and its gnarled hands and fingers, it stood an aged, stern, and scornful monster among the smiling birch trees. Only the dead-looking evergreen firs dotted about in the forest, and this oak, refused to yield to the charm of spring or notice either the spring or the sunshine.

"Spring, love, happiness!" this oak seemed to say. "Are you not weary of that stupid, meaningless, constantly repeated fraud? Always the same and always a fraud? There is no spring, no sun, no happiness! Look at those cramped dead firs, ever the same, and at me too, sticking out my broken and barked fingers just where they have grown, whether from my back or my sides: as they have grown so I stand, and I do not believe in your hopes and your lies."

As he passed through the forest Prince Andrew turned several times to look at that oak, as if expecting something from it. Under the oak, too, were flowers and grass, but it stood among them scowling, rigid, misshapen, and grim as ever.

"Yes, the oak is right, a thousand times right," thought Prince Andrew. "Let others—the young—yield afresh to that fraud, but we know life, our life is finished!"

A whole sequence of new thoughts, hopeless but mournfully pleasant, rose in his soul in connection with that tree. During this journey he, as it were, considered his life afresh and arrived at his old conclusion, restful in its hopelessness: that it was not for him to begin anything anew—but that he must live out his life, content to do no harm, and not disturbing himself or desiring anything.

CHAPTER II

Prince Andrew had to see the Marshal of the Nobility for the district in connection with the affairs of the Ryazán estate of which he was trustee. This Marshal was Count IlyáRostóv, and in the middle of May Prince Andrew went to visit him.

It was now hot spring weather. The whole forest was already clothed in green. It was dusty and so hot that on passing near water one longed to bathe.

Prince Andrew, depressed and preoccupied with the business about which he had to speak to the Marshal, was driving up the avenue in the grounds of the Rostóvs' house at Otrádnoe. He heard merry girlish cries behind some trees on the right and saw a group of girls running to cross the path of his *calèche*. Ahead of the rest and nearer to him ran a dark-haired, remarkably slim, pretty girl in a yellow chintz dress, with a white handkerchief on her head from under which loose locks of hair escaped. The girl was shouting something but, seeing that he was a stranger, ran back laughing without looking at him.

Suddenly, he did not know why, he felt a pang. The day was so beautiful, the sun so bright, everything around so gay, but that slim pretty girl did not know, or wish to know, of his existence and was contented and cheerful in her own separate—probably foolish—but bright and happy life. "What is she so glad about? What is she thinking of? Not of the military regulations or of the arrangement of the Ryazán serfs' quitrents. Of what is she thinking? Why is she so happy?" Prince Andrew asked himself with instinctive curiosity.

In 1809 Count IlyáRostóv was living at Otrádnoe just as he had done in former years, that is, entertaining almost the whole province with hunts, theatricals, dinners, and music. He was glad to see Prince Andrew, as he was to see any new visitor, and insisted on his staying the night.

During the dull day, in the course of which he was entertained by his elderly hosts and by the more important of the visitors (the old count's house was crowded on account of an approaching name day), Prince Andrew repeatedly glanced at Natásha, gay and laughing among the younger members of the company, and asked himself each time, "What is she thinking about? Why is she so glad?"

That night, alone in new surroundings, he was long unable to sleep. He read awhile and then put out his candle, but relit it. It was hot in the room, the inside shutters of which were closed. He was cross with the stupid old man (as he called Rostóv), who had made him stay by assuring him that some necessary documents had not yet arrived from town, and he was vexed with himself for having stayed.

He got up and went to the window to open it. As soon as he opened the shutters the moonlight, as if it had long been watching for this, burst into the room. He opened the casement. The night was fresh, bright, and very still. Just before the window was a row of pollard trees, looking black on one side and with a silvery light on the other. Beneath the trees grew some kind of lush, wet, bushy vegetation with silver-lit leaves and stems here and there. Farther back beyond the dark trees a roof glittered with dew, to the right was a leafy tree with brilliantly white trunk and branches, and above it shone the moon, nearly at its full, in a pale, almost starless, spring sky. Prince Andrew leaned his elbows on the window ledge and his eyes rested on that sky.

His room was on the first floor. Those in the rooms above were also awake. He heard female voices overhead.

"Just once more," said a girlish voice above him which Prince Andrew recognized at once.

"But when are you coming to bed?" replied another voice.

"I won't, I can't sleep, what's the use? Come now for the last time."

Two girlish voices sang a musical passage—the end of some song.

"Oh, how lovely! Now go to sleep, and there's an end of it."

"You go to sleep, but I can't," said the first voice, coming nearer to the window. She was evidently leaning right out, for the rustle of her dress and even her breathing could be heard. Everything was stone-still, like the moon and its light and the shadows. Prince Andrew, too, dared not stir, for fear of betraying his unintentional presence.

"Sónya! Sónya!" he again heard the first speaker. "Oh, how can you sleep? Only look how glorious it is! Ah, how glorious! Do wake up, Sónya!" she said almost with tears in her voice. "There never, never was such a lovely night before!"

Sónya made some reluctant reply.

"Do just come and see what a moon!... Oh, how lovely! Come here.... Darling, sweetheart, come here! There, you see? I feel like sitting down on my heels, putting my arms round my knees like this, straining tight, as tight as possible, and flying away! Like this...."

"Take care, you'll fall out."

He heard the sound of a scuffle and Sónya's disapproving voice: "It's past one o'clock."

"Oh, you only spoil things for me. All right, go, go!"

Again all was silent, but Prince Andrew knew she was still sitting there. From time to time he heard a soft rustle and at times a sigh.

"O God, O God! What does it mean?" she suddenly exclaimed. "To bed then, if it must be!" and she slammed the casement.

"For her I might as well not exist!" thought Prince Andrew while he listened to her voice, for some reason expecting yet fearing that she might say something about him. "There she is again! As if it were on purpose," thought he.

In his soul there suddenly arose such an unexpected turmoil of youthful thoughts and hopes, contrary to the whole tenor of his life, that unable to explain his condition to himself he lay down and fell asleep at once.

CHAPTER III

Next morning, having taken leave of no one but the count, and not waiting for the ladies to appear, Prince Andrew set off for home.

It was already the beginning of June when on his return journey he drove into the birch forest where the gnarled old oak had made so strange and memorable an impression on him. In the forest the harness bells sounded yet more muffled than they had done six weeks before, for now all was thick, shady, and dense, and the young firs dotted about in the forest did not jar on the general beauty but, lending themselves to the mood around, were delicately green with fluffy young shoots.

The whole day had been hot. Somewhere a storm was gathering, but only a small cloud had scattered some raindrops lightly, sprinkling the road and the sappy leaves. The left side of the forest was dark in the shade, the right side glittered in the sunlight, wet and shiny and scarcely swayed by the breeze. Everything was in blossom, the nightingales trilled, and their voices reverberated now near, now far away.

"Yes, here in this forest was that oak with which I agreed," thought Prince Andrew. "But where is it?" he again wondered, gazing at the left side of the road, and without recognizing it he looked with admiration at the very oak he sought. The old oak, quite transfigured, spreading out a canopy of sappy dark-green foliage, stood rapt and slightly trembling in the rays of the evening sun. Neither gnarled fingers nor old scars nor old doubts and sorrows were any of them in evidence now. Through the hard century-old bark, even where there were no twigs, leaves had sprouted such as one could hardly believe the old veteran could have produced.

"Yes, it is the same oak," thought Prince Andrew, and all at once he was seized by an unreasoning springtime feeling of joy and renewal. All the best moments of his life suddenly rose to his memory. Austerlitz with the lofty heavens, his wife's dead reproachful face, Pierre at the ferry, that girl thrilled by the beauty of the night, and that night itself and the moon, and... all this rushed suddenly to his mind.

"No, life is not over at thirty-one!" Prince Andrew suddenly decided finally and decisively. "It is not enough for me to know what I have in me—everyone must know it: Pierre, and that young girl who wanted to fly away into the sky, everyone must know me, so that my life may not be lived for myself alone while others live so apart from it, but so that it may be reflected in them all, and they and I may live in harmony!"

On reaching home Prince Andrew decided to go to Petersburg that autumn and found all sorts of reasons for this decision. A whole series of sensible and logical considerations showing it to be essential for him to go to Petersburg, and even to re-enter the service, kept springing up in his mind. He could not now understand how he could ever even have doubted the necessity of taking an active share in life, just as a month before he had not understood how the idea of leaving the quiet country could ever enter his head. It now seemed clear to him that all his experience of life must be senselessly wasted unless he applied it to some kind of work and again played an active part in life. He did not even remember how formerly, on the strength of similar wretched logical arguments, it had seemed obvious that he would be degrading himself if he now, after the lessons he had had in life, allowed himself to believe in the possibility of being useful and in the possibility of happiness or love. Now reason suggested quite the opposite. After that journey to Ryazán he found the country dull; his former pursuits no longer interested him, and often when sitting alone in his study he got up, went to the mirror, and gazed a long time at his own face. Then he would turn away to the portrait of his dead Lise, who with hair curled *à la grecque* looked tenderly and gaily at him out of the gilt frame. She did not now say those former terrible words to him, but looked simply, merrily, and inquisitively at him. And Prince Andrew, crossing his arms behind him, long paced the room, now frowning, now smiling, as he reflected on those irrational, inexpressible thoughts, secret as a crime, which altered his whole life and were connected with Pierre, with fame, with the girl at the window, the oak, and woman's beauty and love. And if anyone came into his room at such moments he was particularly cold, stern, and above all unpleasantly logical.

"My dear," Princess Mary entering at such a moment would say, "little Nicholas can't go out today, it's very cold."

"If it were hot," Prince Andrew would reply at such times very dryly to his sister, "he could go out in his smock, but as it is cold he must wear warm clothes, which were designed for that purpose. That is what follows from the fact that it is cold; and not that a child who needs fresh air should remain at home," he would add with extreme logic, as if punishing someone for those secret illogical emotions that stirred within him.

At such moments Princess Mary would think how intellectual work dries men up.

CHAPTER IV

Prince Andrew arrived in Petersburg in August, 1809. It was the time when the youthfulSperánski was at the zenith of his fame and his reforms were being pushed forward with the greatest energy. That same August the Emperor was thrown from his *calèche*, injured his leg, and remained three weeks at Peterhof, receiving Speránski every day and no one else. At that time the two famous decrees were being prepared that so agitated society—abolishing court ranks and introducing examinations to qualify for the grades of Collegiate Assessor and State Councilor—and not merely these but a whole state constitution, intended to change the existing order of government in Russia: legal, administrative, and financial, from the Council of State down to the district tribunals. Now those vague liberal dreams with which the Emperor Alexander had ascended the throne, and which he had tried to put into effect with the aid of his associates, Czartoryski, Novosíltsev, Kochubéy, and Strógonov— whom he himself in jest had called his *Comité de salut public*—were taking shape and being realized.

Now all these men were replaced by Speránski on the civil side, and Arakchéev on the military. Soon after his arrival Prince Andrew, as a gentleman of the chamber, presented himself at court and at a levee. The Emperor, though he met him twice, did not favor him with a single word. It had always seemed to Prince Andrew before that he was antipathetic to the Emperor and that the latter disliked his face and personality generally, and in the cold, repellent glance the Emperor gave him, he now found further confirmation of this surmise. The courtiers explained the Emperor's neglect of him by His Majesty's displeasure at Bolkónski's not having served since 1805.

"I know myself that one cannot help one's sympathies and antipathies," thought Prince Andrew, "so it will not do to present my proposal for the reform of the army regulations to the Emperor personally, but the project will speak for itself."

He mentioned what he had written to an old field marshal, a friend of his father's. The field marshal made an appointment to see him, received him graciously, and promised to inform the Emperor. A few days later Prince Andrew received notice that he was to go to see the Minister of War, Count Arakchéev.

On the appointed day Prince Andrew entered Count Arakchéev's waiting room at nine in the morning.

He did not know Arakchéev personally, had never seen him, and all he had heard of him inspired him with but little respect for the man.

"He is Minister of War, a man trusted by the Emperor, and I need not concern myself about his personal qualities: he has been commissioned to consider my project, so he alone can get it adopted," thought Prince Andrew as he waited among a number of important and unimportant people in Count Arakchéev's waiting room.

During his service, chiefly as an adjutant, Prince Andrew had seen the anterooms of many important men, and the different types of such rooms were well known to him. Count Arakchéev's anteroom had quite a special character. The faces of the unimportant people awaiting their turn for an audience showed embarrassment and servility; the faces of those of higher rank expressed a common feeling of awkwardness, covered by a mask of unconcern and ridicule of themselves, their situation, and the person for whom they were waiting. Some walked thoughtfully up and down, others whispered and laughed. Prince Andrew heard the nickname "SílaAndréevich" and the words, "*Uncle* will give it to us hot," in reference to Count Arakchéev. One general (an important personage), evidently feeling offended at having to wait so long, sat crossing and uncrossing his legs and smiling contemptuously to himself.

But the moment the door opened one feeling alone appeared on all faces—that of fear. Prince Andrew for the second time asked the adjutant on duty to take in his name, but received an ironical look and was told that his turn would come in due course. After some others had been shown in and out of the minister's room by the adjutant on duty, an officer who struck Prince Andrew by his humiliated and frightened air was admitted at that terrible door. This officer's audience lasted a long time. Then suddenly the grating sound of a harsh voice was heard from the other side of the door, and the officer—with pale face and trembling lips—came out and passed through the waiting room, clutching his head.

After this Prince Andrew was conducted to the door and the officer on duty said in a whisper, "To the right, at the window."

Prince Andrew entered a plain tidy room and saw at the table a man of forty with a long waist, a long closely cropped head, deep wrinkles, scowling brows above dull greenish-hazel eyes and an overhanging red nose. Arakchéev turned his head toward him without looking at him.

"What is your petition?" asked Arakchéev.

"I am not petitioning, your excellency," returned Prince Andrew quietly.

Arakchéev's eyes turned toward him.

"Sit down," said he. "Prince Bolkónski?"

"I am not petitioning about anything. His Majesty the Emperor has deigned to send your excellency a project submitted by me..."

"You see, my dear sir, I have read your project," interrupted Arakchéev, uttering only the first words amiably and then—again without looking at Prince Andrew—relapsing gradually into a tone of grumbling contempt. "You are proposing new military laws? There are many laws but no one to carry out the old ones. Nowadays everybody designs laws, it is easier writing than doing."

"I came at His Majesty the Emperor's wish to learn from your excellency how you propose to deal with the memorandum I have presented," said Prince Andrew politely.

"I have endorsed a resolution on your memorandum and sent it to the committee. I do not approve of it," said Arakchéev, rising and taking a paper from his writing table. "Here!" and he handed it to Prince Andrew.

Across the paper was scrawled in pencil, without capital letters, misspelled, and without punctuation: "Unsoundly constructed because resembles an imitation of the French military code and from the Articles of War needlessly deviating."

"To what committee has the memorandum been referred?" inquired Prince Andrew.

"To the Committee on Army Regulations, and I have recommended that your honor should be appointed a member, but without a salary."

Prince Andrew smiled.

"I don't want one."

"A member without salary," repeated Arakchéev. "I have the honor... Eh! Call the next one! Who else is there?" he shouted, bowing to Prince Andrew.

CHAPTER V

While waiting for the announcement of his appointment to the committee Prince Andrew looked up his former acquaintances, particularly those he knew to be in power and whose aid he might need. In Petersburg he now experienced the same feeling he had had on the eve of a battle, when troubled by anxious curiosity and irresistibly attracted to the ruling circles where the future, on which the fate of millions depended, was being shaped. From the irritation of the older men, the curiosity of the uninitiated, the reserve of the initiated, the hurry and preoccupation of everyone, and the innumerable committees and commissions of whose existence he learned every day, he felt that now, in 1809, here in Petersburg a vast civil conflict was in preparation, the commander in chief of which was a mysterious person he did not know, but who was supposed to be a man of genius—Speránski. And this movement of reconstruction of which Prince Andrew had a vague idea, and Speránski its chief promoter, began to interest him so keenly that the question of the army regulations quickly receded to a secondary place in his consciousness.

Prince Andrew was most favorably placed to secure good reception in the highest and most diverse Petersburg circles of the day. The reforming party cordially welcomed and courted him, in the first place because he was reputed to be clever and very well read, and secondly because by liberating his serfs he had obtained the reputation of being a liberal. The party of the old and dissatisfied, who censured the innovations, turned to him expecting his sympathy in their disapproval of the reforms, simply because he was the son of his father. The feminine society world welcomed him gladly, because he was rich, distinguished, a good match, and almost a newcomer, with a halo of romance on account of his supposed death and the tragic loss of his wife. Besides this the general opinion of all who had known him previously was that he had greatly improved during these last five years, having softened and grown more manly, lost his former affectation, pride, and contemptuous irony, and acquired the serenity that comes with years. People talked about him, were interested in him, and wanted to meet him.

The day after his interview with Count Arakchéev, Prince Andrew spent the evening at Count Kochubéy's. He told the count of his interview with *SílaAndréevich* (Kochubéyspoke of Arakchéev by that nickname with the same vague irony Prince Andrew had noticed in the Minister of War's anteroom).

"*Mon cher*, even in this case you can't do without Michael MikháylovichSperánski. He manages everything. I'll speak to him. He has promised to come this evening."

"What has Speránski to do with the army regulations?" asked Prince Andrew.

Kochubéy shook his head smilingly, as if surprised at Bolkónski's simplicity.

"We were talking to him about you a few days ago," Kochubéy continued, "and about your freed plowmen."

"Oh, is it you, Prince, who have freed your serfs?" said an old man of Catherine's day, turning contemptuously toward Bolkónski.

"It was a small estate that brought in no profit," replied Prince Andrew, trying to extenuate his action so as not to irritate the old man uselessly.

"Afraid of being late..." said the old man, looking at Kochubéy.

"There's one thing I don't understand," he continued. "Who will plow the land if they are set free? It is easy to write laws, but difficult to rule.... Just the same as now—I ask you, Count—who will be heads of the departments when everybody has to pass examinations?"

"Those who pass the examinations, I suppose," replied Kochubéy, crossing his legs and glancing round.

"Well, I have Pryánichnikov serving under me, a splendid man, a priceless man, but he's sixty. Is he to go up for examination?"

"Yes, that's a difficulty, as education is not at all general, but..."

Count Kochubéy did not finish. He rose, took Prince Andrew by the arm, and went to meet a tall, bald, fair man of about forty with a large open forehead and a long face of unusual and peculiar whiteness, who was just entering. The newcomer wore a blue swallow-tail coat with a cross suspended from his neck and a star on his left breast. It was Speránski. Prince Andrew recognized him at once, and felt a throb within him, as happens at critical moments of life. Whether it was from respect, envy, or anticipation, he did not know. Speránski's whole figure was of a peculiar type that made him easily recognizable. In the society in which Prince Andrew lived he had never seen anyone who together with awkward and clumsy gestures possessed such calmness and self-assurance; he had never seen so resolute yet gentle an expression as that in those half-closed, rather humid eyes, or so firm a smile that expressed nothing; nor had he heard such a refined, smooth, soft voice; above all he had never seen such delicate whiteness of face or hands—hands which were broad, but very plump, soft, and white. Such whiteness and softness Prince Andrew had only seen on the faces of soldiers who had been long in hospital. This was Speránski, Secretary of State, reporter to the Emperor and his companion at Erfurt, where he had more than once met and talked with Napoleon.

Speránski did not shift his eyes from one face to another as people involuntarily do on entering a large company and was in no hurry to speak. He spoke slowly, with assurance that he would be listened to, and he looked only at the person with whom he was conversing.

Prince Andrew followed Speránski's every word and movement with particular attention. As happens to some people, especially to men who judge those near to them severely, he always on meeting anyone new—especially anyone whom, like Speránski, he knew by reputation—expected to discover in him the perfection of human qualities.

Speránski told Kochubéy he was sorry he had been unable to come sooner as he had been detained at the palace. He did not say that the Emperor had kept him, and Prince Andrew noticed this affectation of modesty. When Kochubéy introduced Prince Andrew, Speránski slowly turned his eyes to Bolkónski with his customary smile and looked at him in silence.

"I am very glad to make your acquaintance. I had heard of you, as everyone has," he said after a pause.

Kochubéy said a few words about the reception Arakchéev had given Bolkónski. Speránski smiled more markedly.

"The chairman of the Committee on Army Regulations is my good friend Monsieur Magnítski," he said, fully articulating every word and syllable, "and if you like I can put you in touch with him." He paused at the full stop. "I hope you will find him sympathetic and ready to co-operate in promoting all that is reasonable."

A circle soon formed round Speránski, and the old man who had talked about his subordinate Pryánichnikov addressed a question to him.

Prince Andrew without joining in the conversation watched every movement of Speránski's: this man, not long since an insignificant divinity student, who now, Bolkónski thought, held in his hands—those plump white hands—the fate of Russia. Prince Andrew was struck by the extraordinarily disdainful composure with which Speránski answered the old man. He appeared to address condescending words to him from an immeasurable height. When the old man began to speak too loud, Speránski smiled and said he could not judge of the advantage or disadvantage of what pleased the sovereign.

Having talked for a little while in the general circle, Speránski rose and coming up to Prince Andrew took him along to the other end of the room. It was clear that he thought it necessary to interest himself in Bolkónski.

"I had no chance to talk with you, Prince, during the animated conversation in which that venerable gentleman involved me," he said with a mildly contemptuous smile, as if intimating by that smile that he and Prince Andrew understood the insignificance of the people with whom he had just been talking. This flattered Prince Andrew. "I have known of you for a long time: first from your action with regard to your serfs, a first example, of which it is very desirable that there should be more imitators; and secondly because you are one of those gentlemen of the chamber who have not considered themselves offended by the new decree concerning the ranks allotted to courtiers, which is causing so much gossip and tittle-tattle."

"No," said Prince Andrew, "my father did not wish me to take advantage of the privilege. I began the service from the lower grade."

"Your father, a man of the last century, evidently stands above our contemporaries who so condemn this measure which merely re-establishes natural justice."

"I think, however, that these condemnations have some ground," returned Prince Andrew, trying to resist Speránski's influence, of which he began to be conscious. He did not like to agree with him in everything and felt a wish to contradict. Though he usually spoke easily and well, he felt a difficulty in expressing himself now while talking with Speránski. He was too much absorbed in observing the famous man's personality.

"Grounds of personal ambition maybe," Speránski put in quietly.

"And of state interest to some extent," said Prince Andrew.

"What do you mean?" asked Speránski quietly, lowering his eyes.

"I am an admirer of Montesquieu," replied Prince Andrew, "and his idea that *le principe des monarchies estl'honneur me paraîtincontestable. Certains droits et privilèges de la noblesse me paraissentêtre des moyens de soutenirce sentiment.*" *

* "The principle of monarchies is honor seems to me incontestable. Certain rights and privileges for the aristocracy appear to me a means of maintaining that sentiment."

The smile vanished from Speránski's white face, which was much improved by the change. Probably Prince Andrew's thought interested him.

"*Si vousenvisagez la question sous ce point de vue,*" * he began, pronouncing French with evident difficulty, and speaking even slower than in Russian but quite calmly.

* "If you regard the question from that point of view."

Speránski went on to say that honor, *l'honneur*, cannot be upheld by privileges harmful to the service; that honor, *l'honneur*, is either a negative concept of not doing what is blameworthy or it is a source of emulation in pursuit of commendation and rewards, which recognize it. His arguments were concise, simple, and clear.

"An institution upholding honor, the source of emulation, is one similar to the *Légion d'honneur* of the great Emperor Napoleon, not harmful but helpful to the success of the service, but not a class or court privilege."

"I do not dispute that, but it cannot be denied that court privileges have attained the same end," returned Prince Andrew. "Every courtier considers himself bound to maintain his position worthily."

"Yet you do not care to avail yourself of the privilege, Prince," said Speránski, indicating by a smile that he wished to finish amiably an argument which was embarrassing for his companion. "If you will do me the honor of calling on me on Wednesday," he added, "I will, after talking with Magnítski, let you know what may interest you, and shall also have the pleasure of a more detailed chat with you."

Closing his eyes, he bowed *à la française*, without taking leave, and trying to attract as little attention as possible, he left the room.

CHAPTER VI

During the first weeks of his stay in Petersburg Prince Andrew felt the whole trend of thought he had formed during his life of seclusion quite overshadowed by the trifling cares that engrossed him in that city.

On returning home in the evening he would jot down in his notebook four or five necessary calls or appointments for certain hours. The mechanism of life, the arrangement of the day so as to be in time everywhere, absorbed the greater part of his vital energy. He did nothing, did not even think or find time to think, but only talked, and talked successfully, of what he had thought while in the country.

He sometimes noticed with dissatisfaction that he repeated the same remark on the same day in different circles. But he was so busy for whole days together that he had no time to notice that he was thinking of nothing.

As he had done on their first meeting at Kochubéy's, Speránski produced a strong impression on Prince Andrew on the Wednesday, when he received him tête-à-tête at his own house and talked to him long and confidentially.

To Bolkónski so many people appeared contemptible and insignificant creatures, and he so longed to find in someone the living ideal of that perfection toward which he strove, that he readily believed that in Speránski he had found this ideal of a perfectly rational and virtuous man. Had Speránski sprung from the same class as himself and possessed the same breeding and traditions, Bolkónski would soon have discovered his weak, human, unheroic sides; but as it was, Speránski's strange and logical turn of mind inspired him with respect all the more because he did not quite understand him. Moreover, Speránski, either because he appreciated the other's capacity or because he considered it necessary to win him to his side, showed off his dispassionate calm reasonableness before Prince Andrew and flattered him with that subtle flattery which goes hand in hand with self-assurance and consists in a tacit assumption that one's companion is the only man besides oneself capable of understanding the folly of the rest of mankind and the reasonableness and profundity of one's own ideas.

During their long conversation on Wednesday evening, Speránski more than once remarked: "We regard everything that is above the common level of rooted custom..." or, with a smile: "But *we* want the wolves to be fed and the sheep to be safe..." or: "*They* cannot understand this..." and all in a way that seemed to say: "*We*, you and I, understand what *they* are and who *we* are."

This first long conversation with Speránski only strengthened in Prince Andrew the feeling he had experienced toward him at their first meeting. He saw in him a remarkable, clear-thinking man of vast intellect who by his energy and persistence had attained power, which he was using solely for the welfare of Russia. In Prince Andrew's eyes Speránski was the man he would himself have wished to be—one who explained all the facts of life reasonably, considered important only what was rational, and was capable of applying the standard of reason to everything. Everything seemed so simple and clear in Speránski's exposition that Prince Andrew involuntarily agreed with him about everything. If he replied and argued, it was only because he wished to maintain his independence and not submit to Speránski's opinions entirely. Everything was right and everything was as it should be: only one thing disconcerted Prince Andrew. This was Speránski's cold, mirrorlike look, which did not allow one to penetrate to his soul, and his delicate white hands, which Prince Andrew involuntarily watched as one does watch the hands of those who possess power. This mirrorlike gaze and those delicate hands irritated Prince Andrew, he knew not why. He was unpleasantly struck, too, by the excessive contempt for others that he observed in Speránski, and by the diversity of lines of argument he used to support his opinions. He made use of every kind of mental device, except analogy, and passed too boldly, it seemed to Prince Andrew, from one to another. Now he would take up the position of a practical man and condemn dreamers; now that of a satirist, and laugh ironically at his opponents; now grow severely logical, or suddenly rise to the realm of metaphysics. (This last resource was one he very frequently employed.) He would transfer a question to metaphysical heights, pass on to definitions of space, time, and thought, and, having deduced the refutation he needed, would again descend to the level of the original discussion.

In general the trait of Speránski's mentality which struck Prince Andrew most was his absolute and unshakable belief in the power and authority of reason. It was evident that the thought could never occur to him which to Prince Andrew seemed so natural, namely, that it is after all impossible to express all one thinks; and that he had never felt the doubt, "Is not all I think and believe nonsense?" And it was just this peculiarity of Speránski's mind that particularly attracted Prince Andrew.

During the first period of their acquaintance Bolkónski felt a passionate admiration for him similar to that which he had once felt for Bonaparte. The fact that Speránski was the son of a village priest, and that stupid people might meanly despise him on account of his humble origin (as in fact many did), caused Prince Andrew to cherish his sentiment for him the more, and unconsciously to strengthen it.

On that first evening Bolkónski spent with him, having mentioned the Commission for the Revision of the Code of Laws, Speránski told him sarcastically that the Commission had existed for a hundred and fifty years, had cost millions, and had done nothing except that Rosenkampf had stuck labels on the corresponding paragraphs of the different codes.

"And that is all the state has for the millions it has spent," said he. "We want to give the Senate new juridical powers, but we have no laws. That is why it is a sin for men like you, Prince, not to serve in these times!"

Prince Andrew said that for that work an education in jurisprudence was needed which he did not possess.

"But nobody possesses it, so what would you have? It is a vicious circle from which we must break a way out."

A week later Prince Andrew was a member of the Committee on Army Regulations and—what he had not at all expected—was chairman of a section of the committee for the revision of the laws. At Speránski's request he took the first part of the Civil Code that was being drawn up and, with the aid of the *Code Napoléon* and the Institutes of Justinian, he worked at formulating the section on Personal Rights.

CHAPTER VII

Nearly two years before this, in 1808, Pierre on returning to Petersburg after visiting his estates had involuntarily found himself in a leading position among the Petersburg Freemasons. He arranged dining and funeral lodge meetings, enrolled new members, and busied himself uniting various lodges and acquiring authentic charters. He gave money for the erection of temples and supplemented as far as he could the collection of alms, in regard to which the majority of members were stingy and irregular. He supported almost singlehanded a poorhouse the order had founded in Petersburg.

His life meanwhile continued as before, with the same infatuations and dissipations. He liked to dine and drink well, and though he considered it immoral and humiliating could not resist the temptations of the bachelor circles in which he moved.

Amid the turmoil of his activities and distractions, however, Pierre at the end of a year began to feel that the more firmly he tried to rest upon it, the more Masonic ground on which he stood gave way under him. At the same time he felt that the deeper the ground sank under him the closer bound he involuntarily became to the order. When he had joined the Freemasons he had experienced the feeling of one who confidently steps onto the smooth surface of a bog. When he put his foot down it sank in. To make quite sure of the firmness of the ground, he put his other foot down and sank deeper still, became stuck in it, and involuntarily waded knee-deep in the bog.

Joseph Alexéevich was not in Petersburg—he had of late stood aside from the affairs of the Petersburg lodges, and lived almost entirely in Moscow. All the members of the lodges were men Pierre knew in ordinary life, and it was difficult for him to regard them merely as Brothers in Freemasonry and not as Prince B. or Iván Vasílevich D., whom he knew in society mostly as weak and insignificant men. Under the Masonic aprons and insignia he saw the uniforms and decorations at which they aimed in ordinary life. Often after collecting alms, and reckoning up twenty to thirty rubles received for the most part in promises from a dozen members, of whom half were as well able to pay as himself, Pierre remembered the Masonic vow in which each Brother promised to devote all his belongings to his neighbor, and doubts on which he tried not to dwell arose in his soul.

He divided the Brothers he knew into four categories. In the first he put those who did not take an active part in the affairs of the lodges or in human affairs, but were exclusively occupied with the mystical science of the order: with questions of the threefold designation of God, the three primordial elements—sulphur, mercury, and salt—or the meaning of the square and all the various figures of the temple of Solomon. Pierre respected this class of Brothers to which the elder ones chiefly belonged, including, Pierre thought, Joseph Alexéevich himself, but he did not share their interests. His heart was not in the mystical aspect of Freemasonry.

In the second category Pierre reckoned himself and others like him, seeking and vacillating, who had not yet found in Freemasonry a straight and comprehensible path, but hoped to do so.

In the third category he included those Brothers (the majority) who saw nothing in Freemasonry but the external forms and ceremonies, and prized the strict performance of these forms without troubling about their purport or significance. Such were Willarski and even the Grand Master of the principal lodge.

Finally, to the fourth category also a great many Brothers belonged, particularly those who had lately joined. These according to Pierre's observations were men who had no belief in anything, nor desire for anything, but joined the Freemasons merely to associate with the wealthy young Brothers who were influential through their connections or rank, and of whom there were very many in the lodge.

Pierre began to feel dissatisfied with what he was doing. Freemasonry, at any rate as he saw it here, sometimes seemed to him based merely on externals. He did not think of doubting Freemasonry itself, but suspected that Russian Masonry had taken a wrong path and deviated from its original principles. And so toward the end of the year he went abroad to be initiated into the higher secrets of the order.

In the summer of 1809 Pierre returned to Petersburg. Our Freemasons knew from correspondence with those abroad that Bezúkhov had obtained the confidence of many highly placed persons, had been initiated into many mysteries, had been raised to a higher grade, and was bringing back with him much that might conduce to the advantage of the Masonic cause in Russia. The Petersburg Freemasons all came to see him, tried to ingratiate themselves with him, and it seemed to them all that he was preparing something for them and concealing it.

A solemn meeting of the lodge of the second degree was convened, at which Pierre promised to communicate to the Petersburg Brothers what he had to deliver to them from the highest leaders of their order. The meeting was a full one. After the usual ceremonies Pierre rose and began his address.

"Dear Brothers," he began, blushing and stammering, with a written speech in his hand, "it is not sufficient to observe our mysteries in the seclusion of our lodge—we must act—act! We are drowsing, but we must act." Pierre raised his notebook and began to read.

"For the dissemination of pure truth and to secure the triumph of virtue," he read, "we must cleanse men from prejudice, diffuse principles in harmony with the spirit of the times, undertake the education of the young, unite ourselves in indissoluble bonds with the wisest men, boldly yet prudently overcome superstitions, infidelity, and folly, and form of those devoted to us a body linked together by unity of purpose and possessed of authority and power.

"To attain this end we must secure a preponderance of virtue over vice and must endeavor to secure that the honest man may, even in this world, receive a lasting reward for his virtue. But in these great endeavors we are gravely hampered by the political institutions of today. What is to be done in these circumstances? To favor revolutions, overthrow everything, repel force by force?... No! We are very far from that. Every violent reform deserves censure, for it quite fails to remedy evil while men remain what they are, and also because wisdom needs no violence.

"The whole plan of our order should be based on the idea of preparing men of firmness and virtue bound together by unity of conviction—aiming at the punishment of vice and folly, and patronizing talent and virtue: raising worthy men from the dust and attaching them to our Brotherhood. Only then will our order have the power unobtrusively to bind the hands of the protectors of disorder and to control them without their being aware of it. In a word, we must found a form of government holding universal sway, which should be diffused over the whole world without destroying the bonds of citizenship, and beside which all other governments can continue in their customary course and do everything except what impedes the great aim of our order, which is to obtain for virtue the victory over vice. This aim was that of Christianity itself. It taught men to be wise and good and for their own benefit to follow the example and instruction of the best and wisest men.

"At that time, when everything was plunged in darkness, preaching alone was of course sufficient. The novelty of Truth endowed her with special strength, but now we need much more powerful methods. It is now necessary that man, governed by his senses, should find in virtue a charm palpable to those senses. It is impossible to eradicate the passions; but we must strive to direct them to a noble aim, and it is therefore necessary that everyone should be able to satisfy his passions within the limits of virtue. Our order should provide means to that end.

"As soon as we have a certain number of worthy men in every state, each of them again training two others and all being closely united, everything will be possible for our order, which has already in secret accomplished much for the welfare of mankind."

This speech not only made a strong impression, but created excitement in the lodge. The majority of the Brothers, seeing in it dangerous designs of Illuminism, * met it with a coldness that surprised Pierre. The Grand Master began answering him, and Pierre began developing his views with more and more warmth. It was long since there had been so stormy a meeting. Parties were formed, some accusing Pierre of Illuminism, others supporting him. At that meeting he was struck for the first time by the endless variety of men's minds, which prevents a truth from ever presenting itself identically to two persons. Even those members who seemed to be on his side understood him in their own way with limitations and alterations he could not agree to, as what he always wanted most was to convey his thought to others just as he himself understood it.

* The Illuminati sought to substitute republican for monarchical institutions.

At the end of the meeting the Grand Master with irony and ill-will reproved Bezúkhov for his vehemence and said it was not love of virtue alone, but also a love of strife that had moved him in the dispute. Pierre did not answer him and asked briefly whether his proposal would be accepted. He was told that it would not, and without waiting for the usual formalities he left the lodge and went home.

CHAPTER VIII

Again Pierre was overtaken by the depression he so dreaded. For three days after the delivery of his speech at the lodge he lay on a sofa at home receiving no one and going nowhere.

It was just then that he received a letter from his wife, who implored him to see her, telling him how grieved she was about him and how she wished to devote her whole life to him.

At the end of the letter she informed him that in a few days she would return to Petersburg from abroad.

Following this letter one of the Masonic Brothers whom Pierre respected less than the others forced his way in to see him and, turning the conversation upon Pierre's matrimonial affairs, by way of fraternal advice expressed the opinion that his severity to his wife was wrong and that he was neglecting one of the first rules of Freemasonry by not forgiving the penitent.

At the same time his mother-in-law, Prince Vasíli's wife, sent to him imploring him to come if only for a few minutes to discuss a most important matter. Pierre saw that there was a conspiracy against him and that they wanted to reunite him with his wife, and in the mood he then was, this was not even unpleasant to him. Nothing mattered to him. Nothing in life seemed to him of much importance, and under the influence of the depression that possessed him he valued neither his liberty nor his resolution to punish his wife.

"No one is right and no one is to blame; so she too is not to blame," he thought.

If he did not at once give his consent to a reunion with his wife, it was only because in his state of depression he did not feel able to take any step. Had his wife come to him, he would not have turned her away. Compared to what preoccupied him, was it not a matter of indifference whether he lived with his wife or not?

Without replying either to his wife or his mother-in-law, Pierre late one night prepared for a journey and started for Moscow to see Joseph Alexéevich. This is what he noted in his diary:

Moscow, 17th November

I have just returned from my benefactor, and hasten to write down what I have experienced. Joseph Alexéevich is living poorly and has for three years been suffering from a painful disease of the bladder. No one has ever heard him utter a groan or a word of complaint. From morning till late at night, except when he eats his very plain food, he is working at science. He received me graciously and made me sit down on the bed on which he lay. I made the sign of the Knights of the East and of Jerusalem, and he responded in the same manner, asking me with a mild smile what I had learned and gained in the Prussian and Scottish lodges. I told him everything as best I could, and told him what I had proposed to our Petersburg lodge, of the bad reception I had encountered, and of my rupture with the Brothers. Joseph Alexéevich, having remained silent and thoughtful for a good while, told me his view of the matter, which at once lit up for me my whole past and the future path I should follow. He surprised me by asking whether I remembered the threefold aim of the order: (1) The preservation and study of the mystery. (2) The purification and reformation of oneself for its reception, and (3) The improvement of the human race by striving for such purification. Which is the principal *aim* of these three? Certainly self-reformation and self-purification. Only to this aim can we always strive independently of circumstances. But at the same time just this aim demands the greatest efforts of us; and so, led astray by pride, losing sight of this aim, we occupy ourselves either with the mystery which in our impurity we are unworthy to receive, or seek the reformation of the human race while ourselves setting an example of baseness and profligacy. Illuminism is not a pure doctrine, just because it is attracted by social activity and puffed up by pride. On this ground Joseph Alexéevich condemned my speech and my whole activity, and in the depth of my soul I agreed with him. Talking of my family affairs he said to me, "the chief duty of a true Mason, as I have told you, lies in perfecting himself. We often think that by removing all the difficulties of our life we shall more quickly reach our aim, but on the contrary, my dear sir, it is only in the midst of worldly cares that we can attain our three chief aims: (1) Self-knowledge—for man can only know himself by comparison, (2) Self-perfecting, which can only be attained by conflict, and (3) The attainment of the chief virtue—love of death. Only the vicissitudes of life can show us its vanity and develop our innate love of death or of rebirth to a new life." These words are all the more remarkable because, in spite of his great physical sufferings, Joseph Alexéevich is never weary of life though he loves death, for which—in spite of the purity and loftiness of his inner man—he does not yet feel himself sufficiently prepared. My benefactor then explained to me fully the meaning of the Great Square of creation and pointed out to me that the numbers three and seven are the basis of everything. He advised me not to avoid intercourse with the Petersburg Brothers, but to take up only second-grade posts in the lodge, to try, while diverting the Brothers from pride, to turn them toward the true path self-knowledge and self-perfecting. Besides this he advised me for myself personally above all to keep a watch over myself, and to that end he gave me a notebook, the one I am now writing in and in which I will in future note down all my actions.

Petersburg, 23rd November

I am again living with my wife. My mother-in-law came to me in tears and said that Hélène was here and that she implored me to hear her; that she was innocent and unhappy at my desertion, and much more. I knew that if I once let myself see her I should not have strength to go on refusing what she wanted. In my perplexity I did not know whose aid and advice to seek. Had my benefactor been here he would have told me what to do. I went to my room and reread Joseph Alexéevich's letters and recalled my conversations with him, and deduced from it all that I ought not to refuse a supplicant, and ought to reach a helping hand to everyone—especially to one so closely bound to me—and that I must bear my cross. But if I forgive her for the sake of doing right, then let union with her have only a spiritual aim. That is what I decided, and what I wrote to Joseph Alexéevich. I told my wife that I begged her to forget the past, to forgive me whatever wrong I may have done her, and that I had nothing to forgive. It gave me joy to tell her this. She need not know how hard it was for me to see her again. I have settled on the upper floor of this big house and am experiencing a happy feeling of regeneration.

CHAPTER IX

At that time, as always happens, the highest society that met at court and at the grand balls was divided into several circles, each with its own particular tone. The largest of these was the French circle of the Napoleonic alliance, the circle of Count Rumyántsev and Caulaincourt. In this group Hélène, as soon as she had settled in Petersburg with her husband, took a very prominent place. She was visited by the members of the French embassy and by many belonging to that circle and noted for their intellect and polished manners.

Hélène had been at Erfurt during the famous meeting of the Emperors and had brought from there these connections with the Napoleonic notabilities. At Erfurt her success had been brilliant. Napoleon himself had noticed her in the theater and said of her: *"C'est un superbe animal."* * Her success as a beautiful and elegant woman did not surprise Pierre, for she had become even handsomer than before. What did surprise him was that during these last two years his wife had succeeded in gaining the reputation *"d' une femme charmante, aussi spirituelle que belle."* *(2) The distinguished Prince de Ligne wrote her eight-page letters. Bilíbin saved up his epigrams to produce them in Countess Bezúkhova's presence. To be received in the Countess Bezúkhova's salon was regarded as a diploma of intellect. Young men read books before attending Hélène's evenings, to have something to say in her salon, and secretaries of the embassy, and even ambassadors, confided diplomatic secrets to her, so that in a way Hélène was a power. Pierre, who knew she was very stupid, sometimes attended, with a strange feeling of perplexity and fear, her evenings and dinner parties, where politics, poetry, and philosophy were discussed. At these parties his feelings were like those of a conjuror who always expects his trick to be found out at any moment. But whether because stupidity was just what was needed to run such a salon, or because those who were deceived found pleasure in the deception, at any rate it remained unexposed and Hélène Bezúkhova's reputation as a lovely and clever woman became so firmly established that she could say the emptiest and stupidest things and everybody would go into raptures over every word of hers and look for a profound meaning in it of which she herself had no conception.

* "That's a superb animal."

* (2) "Of a charming woman, as witty as she is lovely."

Pierre was just the husband needed for a brilliant society woman. He was that absent-minded crank, a *grand seigneur* husband who was in no one's way, and far from spoiling the high tone and general impression of the drawing room, he served, by the contrast he presented to her, as an advantageous background to his elegant and tactful wife. Pierre during the last two years, as a result of his continual absorption in abstract interests and his sincere contempt for all else, had acquired in his wife's circle, which did not interest him, that air of unconcern, indifference, and benevolence toward all, which cannot be acquired artificially and therefore inspires involuntary respect. He entered his wife's drawing room as one enters a theater, was acquainted with everybody, equally pleased to see everyone, and equally indifferent to them all. Sometimes he joined in a conversation which interested him and, regardless of whether any "gentlemen of the embassy" were present or not, lispingly expressed his views, which were sometimes not at all in accord with the accepted tone of the moment. But the general opinion concerning the queer husband of "the most distinguished woman in Petersburg" was so well established that no one took his freaks seriously.

Among the many young men who frequented her house every day, BorísDrubetskóy, who had already achieved great success in the service, was the most intimate friend of the Bezúkhov household since Hélène's return from Erfurt. Hélène spoke of him as *"mon page"* and treated him like a child. Her smile for him was the same as for everybody, but sometimes that smile made Pierre uncomfortable. Toward him Borís behaved with a particularly dignified and sad deference. This shade of deference also disturbed Pierre. He had suffered so painfully three years before from the mortification to which his wife had subjected him that he now protected himself from the danger of its repetition, first by not being a husband to his wife, and secondly by not allowing himself to suspect.

"No, now that she has become a bluestocking she has finally renounced her former infatuations," he told himself. "There has never been an instance of a bluestocking being carried away by affairs of the heart"—a statement which, though gathered from an unknown source, he believed implicitly. Yet strange to say Borís' presence in his wife's drawing room (and he was almost always there) had a physical effect upon Pierre; it constricted his limbs and destroyed the unconsciousness and freedom of his movements.

"What a strange antipathy," thought Pierre, "yet I used to like him very much."

In the eyes of the world Pierre was a great gentleman, the rather blind and absurd husband of a distinguished wife, a clever crank who did nothing but harmed nobody and was a first-rate, good-natured fellow. But a complex and difficult process of internal development was taking place all this time in Pierre's soul, revealing much to him and causing him many spiritual doubts and joys.

CHAPTER X

Pierre went on with his diary, and this is what he wrote in it during that time:

24th November

Got up at eight, read the Scriptures, then went to my duties. (By Joseph Alexéevich's advice Pierre had entered the service of the state and served on one of the committees.) Returned home for dinner and dined alone—the countess had many visitors I do not like. I ate and drank moderately and after dinner copied out some passages for the Brothers. In the evening I went down to the countess and told a funny story about B., and only remembered that I ought not to have done so when everybody laughed loudly at it.

I am going to bed with a happy and tranquil mind. Great God, help me to walk in Thy paths, (1) to conquer anger by calmness and deliberation, (2) to vanquish lust by self-restraint and repulsion, (3) to withdraw from worldliness, but not avoid (a) the service of the state, (b) family duties, (c) relations with my friends, and the management of my affairs.

27th November

I got up late. On waking I lay long in bed yielding to sloth. O God, help and strengthen me that I may walk in Thy ways! Read the Scriptures, but without proper feeling. Brother Urúsov came and we talked about worldly vanities. He told me of the Emperor's new projects. I began to criticize them, but remembered my rules and my benefactor's words—that a true Freemason should be a zealous worker for the state when his aid is required and a quiet onlooker when not called on to assist. My tongue is my enemy. Brothers G. V. and O. visited me and we had a preliminary talk about the reception of a new Brother. They laid on me the duty of Rhetor. I feel myself weak and unworthy. Then our talk turned to the interpretation of the seven pillars and steps of the Temple, the seven sciences, the seven virtues, the seven vices, and the seven gifts of the Holy Spirit. Brother O. was very eloquent. In the evening the admission took place. The new decoration of the Premises contributed much to the magnificence of the spectacle. It was Borís Drubetskóy who was admitted. I nominated him and was the Rhetor. A strange feeling agitated me all the time I was alone with him in the dark chamber. I caught myself harboring a feeling of hatred toward him which I vainly tried to overcome. That is why I should really like to save him from evil and lead him into the path of truth, but evil thoughts of him did not leave me. It seemed to me that his object in entering the Brotherhood was merely to be intimate and in favor with members of our lodge. Apart from the fact that he had asked me several times whether N. and S. were members of our lodge (a question to which I could not reply) and that according to my observation he is incapable of feeling respect for our holy order and is too preoccupied and satisfied with the outer man to desire spiritual improvement, I had no cause to doubt him, but he seemed to me insincere, and all the time I stood alone with him in the dark temple it seemed to me that he was smiling contemptuously at my words, and I wished really to stab his bare breast with the sword I held to it. I could not be eloquent, nor could I frankly mention my doubts to the Brothers and to the Grand Master. Great Architect of Nature, help me to find the true path out of the labyrinth of lies!

After this, three pages were left blank in the diary, and then the following was written:

I have had a long and instructive talk alone with Brother V., who advised me to hold fast by Brother A. Though I am unworthy, much was revealed to me. Adonai is the name of the creator of the world. Elohim is the name of the ruler of all. The third name is the name unutterable which means the *All*. Talks with Brother V. strengthen, refresh, and support me in the path of virtue. In his presence doubt has no place. The distinction between the poor teachings of mundane science and our sacred all-embracing teaching is clear to me. Human sciences dissect everything to comprehend it, and kill everything to examine it. In the holy science of our order all is one, all is known in its entirety and life. The Trinity—the three elements of matter—are sulphur, mercury, and salt. Sulphur is of an oily and fiery nature; in combination with salt by its fiery nature it arouses a desire in the latter by means of which it attracts mercury, seizes it, holds it, and in combination produces other bodies. Mercury is a fluid, volatile, spiritual essence. Christ, the Holy Spirit, Him!...

3rd December

Awoke late, read the Scriptures but was apathetic. Afterwards went and paced up and down the large hall. I wished to meditate, but instead my imagination pictured an occurrence of four years ago, when Dólokhov, meeting me in Moscow after our duel, said he hoped I was enjoying perfect peace of mind in spite of my wife's absence. At the time I gave him no answer. Now I recalled every detail of that meeting and in my mind gave him the most malevolent and bitter replies. I recollected myself and drove away that thought only when I found myself glowing with anger, but I did not sufficiently repent. Afterwards BorísDrubetskóy came and began relating various adventures. His coming vexed me from the first, and I said something disagreeable to him. He replied. I flared up and said much that was unpleasant and even rude to him. He became silent, and I recollected myself only when it was too late. My God, I cannot get on with him at all. The cause of this is my egotism. I set myself above him and so become much worse than he, for he is lenient to my rudeness while I on the contrary nourish contempt for him. O God, grant that in his presence I may rather see my own vileness, and behave so that he too may benefit. After dinner I fell asleep and as I was drowsing off I clearly heard a voice saying in my left ear, "Thy day!"

I dreamed that I was walking in the dark and was suddenly surrounded by dogs, but I went on undismayed. Suddenly a smallish dog seized my left thigh with its teeth and would not let go. I began to throttle it with my hands. Scarcely had I torn it off before another, a bigger one, began biting me. I lifted it up, but the higher I lifted it the bigger and heavier it grew. And suddenly Brother A. came and, taking my arm, led me to a building to enter which we had to pass along a narrow plank. I stepped on it, but it bent and gave way and I began to clamber up a fence which I could scarcely reach with my hands. After much effort I dragged myself up, so that my leg hung down on one side and my body on the other. I looked round and saw Brother A. standing on the fence and pointing me to a broad avenue and garden, and in the garden was a large and beautiful building. I woke up. O Lord, great Architect of Nature, help me to tear from myself these dogs—my passions especially the last, which unites in itself the strength of all the former ones, and aid me to enter that temple of virtue to a vision of which I attained in my dream.

7th December

I dreamed that Joseph Alexéevich was sitting in my house, and that I was very glad and wished to entertain him. It seemed as if I chattered incessantly with other people and suddenly remembered that this could not please him, and I wished to come close to him and embrace him. But as soon as I drew near I saw that his face had changed and grown young, and he was quietly telling me something about the teaching of our order, but so softly that I could not hear it. Then it seemed that we all left the room and something strange happened. We were sitting or lying on the floor. He was telling me something, and I wished to show him my sensibility, and not listening to what he was saying I began picturing to myself the condition of my inner man and the grace of God sanctifying me. And tears came into my eyes, and I was glad he noticed this. But he looked at me with vexation and jumped up, breaking off his remarks. I felt abashed and asked whether what he had been saying did not concern me; but he did not reply, gave me a kind look, and then we suddenly found ourselves in my bedroom where there is a double bed. He lay down on the edge of it and I burned with longing to caress him and lie down too. And he said, "Tell me frankly what is your chief temptation? Do you know it? I think you know it already." Abashed by this question, I replied that sloth was my chief temptation. He shook his head incredulously; and even more abashed, I said that though I was living with my wife as he advised, I was not living with her as her husband. To this he replied that one should not deprive a wife of one's embraces and gave me to understand that that was my duty. But I replied that I should be ashamed to do it, and suddenly everything vanished. And I awoke and found in my mind the text from the Gospel: "The life was the light of men. And the light shineth in darkness; and the darkness comprehended it not." Joseph Alexéevich's face had looked young and bright. That day I received a letter from my benefactor in which he wrote about "conjugal duties."

9th December

I had a dream from which I awoke with a throbbing heart. I saw that I was in Moscow in my house, in the big sitting room, and Joseph

Alexéevich came in from the drawing room. I seemed to know at once that the process of regeneration had already taken place in him, and I rushed to meet him. I embraced him and kissed his hands, and he said, "Hast thou noticed that my face is different?" I looked at him, still holding him in my arms, and saw that his face was young, but that he had no hair on his head and his features were quite changed. And I said, "I should have known you had I met you by chance," and I thought to myself, "Am I telling the truth?" And suddenly I saw him lying like a dead body; then he gradually recovered and went with me into my study carrying a large book of sheets of drawing paper; I said, "I drew that," and he answered by bowing his head. I opened the book, and on all the pages there were excellent drawings. And in my dream I knew that these drawings represented the love adventures of the soul with its beloved. And on its pages I saw a beautiful representation of a maiden in transparent garments and with a transparent body, flying up to the clouds. And I seemed to know that this maiden was nothing else than a representation of the Song of Songs. And looking at those drawings I dreamed I felt that I was doing wrong, but could not tear myself away from them. Lord, help me! My God, if Thy forsaking me is Thy doing, Thy will be done; but if I am myself the cause, teach me what I should do! I shall perish of my debauchery if Thou utterly desertest me!

CHAPTER XI

The Rostóvs' monetary affairs had not improved during the two years they had spent in the country.

Though Nicholas Rostóv had kept firmly to his resolution and was still serving modestly in an obscure regiment, spending comparatively little, the way of life at Otrádnoe—Mítenka's management of affairs, in particular—was such that the debts inevitably increased every year. The only resource obviously presenting itself to the old count was to apply for an official post, so he had come to Petersburg to look for one and also, as he said, to let the lassies enjoy themselves for the last time.

Soon after their arrival in Petersburg Berg proposed to Véra and was accepted.

Though in Moscow the Rostóvs belonged to the best society without themselves giving it a thought, yet in Petersburg their circle of acquaintances was a mixed and indefinite one. In Petersburg they were provincials, and the very people they had entertained in Moscow without inquiring to what set they belonged, here looked down on them.

The Rostóvs lived in the same hospitable way in Petersburg as in Moscow, and the most diverse people met at their suppers. Country neighbors from Otrádnoe, impoverished old squires and their daughters, Perónskaya a maid of honor, Pierre Bezúkhov, and the son of their district postmaster who had obtained a post in Petersburg. Among the men who very soon became frequent visitors at the Rostóvs' house in Petersburg were Borís, Pierre whom the count had met in the street and dragged home with him, and Berg who spent whole days at the Rostóvs' and paid the eldest daughter, Countess Véra, the attentions a young man pays when he intends to propose.

Not in vain had Berg shown everybody his right hand wounded at Austerlitz and held a perfectly unnecessary sword in his left. He narrated that episode so persistently and with so important an air that everyone believed in the merit and usefulness of his deed, and he had obtained two decorations for Austerlitz.

In the Finnish war he also managed to distinguish himself. He had picked up the scrap of a grenade that had killed an aide-de-camp standing near the commander in chief and had taken it to his commander. Just as he had done after Austerlitz, he related this occurrence at such length and so insistently that everyone again believed it had been necessary to do this, and he received two decorations for the Finnish war also. In 1809 he was a captain in the Guards, wore medals, and held some special lucrative posts in Petersburg.

Though some skeptics smiled when told of Berg's merits, it could not be denied that he was a painstaking and brave officer, on excellent terms with his superiors, and a moral young man with a brilliant career before him and an assured position in society.

Four years before, meeting a German comrade in the stalls of a Moscow theater, Berg had pointed out VéraRostóva to him and had said in German, *"das sollmeinWeibwerden,"* * and from that moment had made up his mind to marry her. Now in Petersburg, having considered the Rostóvs' position and his own, he decided that the time had come to propose.

* "That girl shall be my wife."

Berg's proposal was at first received with a perplexity that was not flattering to him. At first it seemed strange that the son of an obscure Livonian gentleman should propose marriage to a Countess Rostóva; but Berg's chief characteristic was such a naïve and good natured egotism that the Rostóvs involuntarily came to think it would be a good thing, since he himself was so firmly convinced that it was good, indeed excellent. Moreover, the Rostóvs' affairs were seriously embarrassed, as the suitor could not but know; and above all, Véra was twenty-four, had been taken out everywhere, and though she was certainly good-looking and sensible, no one up to now had proposed to her. So they gave their consent.

"You see," said Berg to his comrade, whom he called "friend" only because he knew that everyone has friends, "you see, I have considered it all, and should not marry if I had not thought it all out or if it were in any way unsuitable. But on the contrary, my papa and mamma are now provided for—I have arranged that rent for them in the Baltic Provinces—and I can live in Petersburg on my pay, and with her fortune and my good management we can get along nicely. I am not marrying for money—I consider that dishonorable—but a wife should bring her share and a husband his. I have my position in the service, she has connections and some means. In our times that is worth something, isn't it? But above all, she is a handsome, estimable girl, and she loves me...."

Berg blushed and smiled.

"And I love her, because her character is sensible and very good. Now the other sister, though they are the same family, is quite different—an unpleasant character and has not the same intelligence. She is so... you know?... Unpleasant... But my fiancée!... Well, you will be coming," he was going to say, "to dine," but changed his mind and said "to take tea with us," and quickly doubling up his tongue he blew a small round ring of tobacco smoke, perfectly embodying his dream of happiness.

After the first feeling of perplexity aroused in the parents by Berg's proposal, the holiday tone of joyousness usual at such times took possession of the family, but the rejoicing was external and insincere. In the family's feeling toward this wedding a certain awkwardness and constraint was evident, as if they were ashamed of not having loved Véra sufficiently and of being so ready to get her off their hands. The old count felt this most. He would probably have been unable to state the cause of his embarrassment, but it resulted from the state of his affairs. He did not know at all how much he had, what his debts amounted to, or what dowry he could give Véra. When his daughters were born he had assigned to each of them, for her dowry, an estate with three hundred serfs; but one of these estates had already been sold, and the other was mortgaged and the interest so much in arrears that it would have to be sold, so that it was impossible to give it to Véra. Nor had he any money.

Berg had already been engaged a month, and only a week remained before the wedding, but the count had not yet decided in his own mind the question of the dowry, nor spoken to his wife about it. At one time the count thought of giving her the Ryazán estate or of selling a forest, at another time of borrowing money on a note of hand. A few days before the wedding Berg entered the count's study early one morning and, with a pleasant smile, respectfully asked his future father-in-law to let him know what Véra's dowry would be. The count was so disconcerted by this long-foreseen inquiry that without consideration he gave the first reply that came into his head. "I like your being businesslike about it.... I like it. You shall be satisfied...."

And patting Berg on the shoulder he got up, wishing to end the conversation. But Berg, smiling pleasantly, explained that if he did not know for certain how much Véra would have and did not receive at least part of the dowry in advance, he would have to break matters off.

"Because, consider, Count—if I allowed myself to marry now without having definite means to maintain my wife, I should be acting badly...."

The conversation ended by the count, who wished to be generous and to avoid further importunity, saying that he would give a note of hand for eighty thousand rubles. Berg smiled meekly, kissed the count on the shoulder, and said that he was very grateful, but that it was impossible for him to arrange his new life without receiving thirty thousand in ready money. "Or at least twenty thousand, Count," he added, "and then a note of hand for only sixty thousand."

"Yes, yes, all right!" said the count hurriedly. "Only excuse me, my dear fellow, I'll give you twenty thousand and a note of hand for eighty thousand as well. Yes, yes! Kiss me."

CHAPTER XII

Natásha was sixteen and it was the year 1809, the very year to which she had counted on her fingers with Borís after they had kissed four years ago. Since then she had not seen him. Before Sónya and her mother, if Borís happened to be mentioned, she spoke quite freely of that episode as of some childish, long-forgotten matter that was not worth mentioning. But in the secret depths of her soul the question whether her engagement to Borís was a jest or an important, binding promise tormented her.

Since Borís left Moscow in 1805 to join the army he had not seen the Rostóvs. He had been in Moscow several times, and had passed near Otrádnoe, but had never been to see them.

Sometimes it occurred to Natásha that he did not wish to see her, and this conjecture was confirmed by the sad tone in which her elders spoke of him.

"Nowadays old friends are not remembered," the countess would say when Borís was mentioned.

Anna Mikháylovna also had of late visited them less frequently, seemed to hold herself with particular dignity, and always spoke rapturously and gratefully of the merits of her son and the brilliant career on which he had entered. When the Rostóvs came to Petersburg Borís called on them.

He drove to their house in some agitation. The memory of Natásha was his most poetic recollection. But he went with the firm intention of letting her and her parents feel that the childish relations between himself and Natásha could not be binding either on her or on him. He had a brilliant position in society thanks to his intimacy with Countess Bezúkhova, a brilliant position in the service thanks to the patronage of an important personage whose complete confidence he enjoyed, and he was beginning to make plans for marrying one of the richest heiresses in Petersburg, plans which might very easily be realized. When he entered the Rostóvs' drawing room Natásha was in her own room. When she heard of his arrival she almost ran into the drawing room, flushed and beaming with a more than cordial smile.

Borís remembered Natásha in a short dress, with dark eyes shining from under her curls and boisterous, childish laughter, as he had known her four years before; and so he was taken aback when quite a different Natásha entered, and his face expressed rapturous astonishment. This expression on his face pleased Natásha.

"Well, do you recognize your little madcap playmate?" asked the countess.

Borís kissed Natásha's hand and said that he was astonished at the change in her.

"How handsome you have grown!"

"I should think so!" replied Natásha's laughing eyes.

"And is Papa older?" she asked.

Natásha sat down and, without joining in Borís' conversation with the countess, silently and minutely studied her childhood's suitor. He felt the weight of that resolute and affectionate scrutiny and glanced at her occasionally.

Borís' uniform, spurs, tie, and the way his hair was brushed were all *comme il faut* and in the latest fashion. This Natásha noticed at once. He sat rather sideways in the armchair next to the countess, arranging with his right hand the cleanest of gloves that fitted his left hand like a skin, and he spoke with a particularly refined compression of his lips about the amusements of the highest Petersburg society, recalling with mild irony old times in Moscow and Moscow acquaintances. It was not accidentally, Natásha felt, that he alluded, when speaking of the highest aristocracy, to an ambassador's ball he had attended, and to invitations he had received from N.N. and S.S.

All this time Natásha sat silent, glancing up at him from under her brows. This gaze disturbed and confused Borís more and more. He looked round more frequently toward her, and broke off in what he was saying. He did not stay more than ten minutes, then rose and took his leave. The same inquisitive, challenging, and rather mocking eyes still looked at him. After his first visit Borís said to himself that Natásha attracted him just as much as ever, but that he must not yield to that feeling, because to marry her, a girl almost without fortune, would mean ruin to his career, while to renew their former relations without intending to marry her would be dishonorable. Borís made up his mind to avoid meeting Natásha, but despite that resolution he called again a few days later and began calling often and spending whole days at the Rostóvs'. It seemed to him that he ought to have an explanation with Natásha and tell her that the old times must be forgotten, that in spite of everything... she could not be his wife, that he had no means, and they would never let her marry him. But he failed to do so and felt awkward about entering on such an explanation. From day to day he became more and more entangled. It seemed to her mother and Sónya that Natásha was in love with Borís as of old. She sang him his favorite songs, showed him her album, making him write in it, did not allow him to allude to the past, letting it be understood how delightful was the present; and every day he went away in a fog, without having said what he meant to, and not knowing what he was doing or why he came, or how it would all end. He left off visiting Hélène and received reproachful notes from her every day, and yet he continued to spend whole days with the Rostóvs.

CHAPTER XIII

One night when the old countess, in nightcap and dressing jacket, without her false curls, and with her poor little knob of hair showing under her white cotton cap, knelt sighing and groaning on a rug and bowing to the ground in prayer, her door creaked and Natásha, also in a dressing jacket with slippers on her bare feet and her hair in curlpapers, ran in. The countess—her prayerful mood dispelled—looked round and frowned. She was finishing her last prayer: "Can it be that this couch will be my grave?" Natásha, flushed and eager, seeing her mother in prayer, suddenly checked her rush, half sat down, and unconsciously put out her tongue as if chiding herself. Seeing that her mother was still praying she ran on tiptoe to the bed and, rapidly slipping one little foot against the other, pushed off her slippers and jumped onto the bed the countess had feared might become her grave. This couch was high, with a feather bed and five pillows each smaller than the one below. Natásha jumped on it, sank into the feather bed, rolled over to the wall, and began snuggling up the bedclothes as she settled down, raising her knees to her chin, kicking out and laughing almost inaudibly, now covering herself up head and all, and now peeping at her mother. The countess finished her prayers and came to the bed with a stern face, but seeing that Natásha's head was covered, she smiled in her kind, weak way.

"Now then, now then!" said she.

"Mamma, can we have a talk? Yes?" said Natásha. "Now, just one on your throat and another... that'll do!" And seizing her mother round the neck, she kissed her on the throat. In her behavior to her mother Natásha seemed rough, but she was so sensitive and tactful that however she clasped her mother she always managed to do it without hurting her or making her feel uncomfortable or displeased.

"Well, what is it tonight?" said the mother, having arranged her pillows and waited until Natásha, after turning over a couple of times, had settled down beside her under the quilt, spread out her arms, and assumed a serious expression.

These visits of Natásha's at night before the count returned from his club were one of the greatest pleasures of both mother, and daughter.

"What is it tonight?—But I have to tell you..."

Natásha put her hand on her mother's mouth.

"About Borís... I know," she said seriously; "that's what I have come about. Don't say it—I know. No, do tell me!" and she removed her hand. "Tell me, Mamma! He's nice?"

"Natásha, you are sixteen. At your age I was married. You say Borís is nice. He is very nice, and I love him like a son. But what then?... What are you thinking about? You have quite turned his head, I can see that...."

As she said this the countess looked round at her daughter. Natásha was lying looking steadily straight before her at one of the mahogany sphinxes carved on the corners of the bedstead, so that the countess only saw her daughter's face in profile. That face struck her by its peculiarly serious and concentrated expression.

Natásha was listening and considering.

"Well, what then?" said she.

"You have quite turned his head, and why? What do you want of him? You know you can't marry him."

"Why not?" said Natásha, without changing her position.

"Because he is young, because he is poor, because he is a relation... and because you yourself don't love him."

"How do you know?"

"I know. It is not right, darling!"

"But if I want to..." said Natásha.

"Leave off talking nonsense," said the countess.

"But if I want to..."

"Natásha, I am in earnest..."

Natásha did not let her finish. She drew the countess' large hand to her, kissed it on the back and then on the palm, then again turned it over and began kissing first one knuckle, then the space between the knuckles, then the next knuckle, whispering, "January, February, March, April, May. Speak, Mamma, why don't you say anything? Speak!" said she, turning to her mother, who was tenderly gazing at her daughter and in that contemplation seemed to have forgotten all she had wished to say.

"It won't do, my love! Not everyone will understand this friendship dating from your childish days, and to see him so intimate with you may injure you in the eyes of other young men who visit us, and above all it torments him for nothing. He may already have found a suitable and wealthy match, and now he's half crazy."

"Crazy?" repeated Natásha.

"I'll tell you some things about myself. I had a cousin..."

"I know! Cyril Matvéich... but he is old."

"He was not always old. But this is what I'll do, Natásha, I'll have a talk with Borís. He need not come so often...."

"Why not, if he likes to?"

"Because I know it will end in nothing...."

"How can you know? No, Mamma, don't speak to him! What nonsense!" said Natásha in the tone of one being deprived of her property. "Well, I won't marry, but let him come if he enjoys it and I enjoy it." Natásha smiled and looked at her mother. "Not to marry, but just so," she added.

"How *so*, my pet?"

"Just *so*. There's no need for me to marry him. But... just *so*."

"Just so, just so," repeated the countess, and shaking all over, she went off into a good humored, unexpected, elderly laugh.

"Don't laugh, stop!" cried Natásha. "You're shaking the whole bed! You're awfully like me, just such another giggler.... Wait..." and she seized the countess' hands and kissed a knuckle of the little finger, saying, "June," and continued, kissing, "July, August," on the other hand. "But, Mamma, is he very much in love? What do you think? Was anybody ever so much in love with you? And he's very nice, very, very nice. Only not quite my taste—he is so narrow, like the dining-room clock.... Don't you understand? Narrow, you know—gray, light gray..."

"What rubbish you're talking!" said the countess.

Natásha continued: "Don't you really understand? Nicholas would understand.... Bezúkhov, now, is blue, dark-blue and red, and he is square."

"You flirt with him too," said the countess, laughing.

"No, he is a Freemason, I have found out. He is fine, dark-blue and red.... How can I explain it to you?"

"Little countess!" the count's voice called from behind the door. "You're not asleep?" Natásha jumped up, snatched up her slippers, and ran barefoot to her own room.

It was a long time before she could sleep. She kept thinking that no one could understand all that she understood and all there was in her.

"Sónya?" she thought, glancing at that curled-up, sleeping little kitten with her enormous plait of hair. "No, how could she? She's virtuous. She fell in love with Nicholas and does not wish to know anything more. Even Mamma does not understand. It is wonderful how clever I am and how... charming she is," she went on, speaking of herself in the third person, and imagining it was some very wise man—the wisest and best of men—who was saying it of her. "There is everything, everything in her," continued this man. "She is unusually intelligent, charming... and then she *is* pretty, uncommonly pretty, and agile—she swims and rides splendidly... and her voice! One can really say it's a wonderful voice!"

She hummed a scrap from her favorite opera by Cherubini, threw herself on her bed, laughed at the pleasant thought that she would immediately fall asleep, called Dunyásha the maid to put out the candle, and before Dunyásha had left the room had already passed into yet another happier world of dreams, where everything was as light and beautiful as in reality, and even more so because it was different.

Next day the countess called Borís aside and had a talk with him, after which he ceased coming to the Rostóvs'.

CHAPTER XIV

On the thirty-first of December, New Year's Eve, 1809 - 10 an old grandee of Catherine's day was giving a ball and midnight supper. The diplomatic corps and the Emperor himself were to be present.

The grandee's well-known mansion on the English Quay glittered with innumerable lights. Police were stationed at the brightly lit entrance which was carpeted with red baize, and not only gendarmes but dozens of police officers and even the police master himself stood at the porch. Carriages kept driving away and fresh ones arriving, with red-liveried footmen and footmen in plumed hats. From the carriages emerged men wearing uniforms, stars, and ribbons, while ladies in satin and ermine cautiously descended the carriage steps which were let down for them with a clatter, and then walked hurriedly and noiselessly over the baize at the entrance.

Almost every time a new carriage drove up a whisper ran through the crowd and caps were doffed.

"The Emperor?... No, a minister... prince... ambassador. Don't you see the plumes?..." was whispered among the crowd.

One person, better dressed than the rest, seemed to know everyone and mentioned by name the greatest dignitaries of the day.

A third of the visitors had already arrived, but the Rostóvs, who were to be present, were still hurrying to get dressed.

There had been many discussions and preparations for this ball in the Rostóv family, many fears that the invitation would not arrive, that the dresses would not be ready, or that something would not be arranged as it should be.

MáryaIgnátevnaPerónskaya, a thin and shallow maid of honor at the court of the Dowager Empress, who was a friend and relation of the countess and piloted the provincial Rostóvs in Petersburg high society, was to accompany them to the ball.

They were to call for her at her house in the Taurida Gardens at ten o'clock, but it was already five minutes to ten, and the girls were not yet dressed.

Natásha was going to her first grand ball. She had got up at eight that morning and had been in a fever of excitement and activity all day. All her powers since morning had been concentrated on ensuring that they all—she herself, Mamma, and Sónya—should be as well dressed as possible. Sónya and her mother put themselves entirely in her hands. The countess was to wear a claret-colored velvet dress, and the two girls white gauze over pink silk slips, with roses on their bodices and their hair dressed *à la grecque*.

Everything essential had already been done; feet, hands, necks, and ears washed, perfumed, and powdered, as befits a ball; the openwork silk stockings and white satin shoes with ribbons were already on; the hairdressing was almost done. Sónya was finishing dressing and so was the countess, but Natásha, who had bustled about helping them all, was behindhand. She was still sitting before a looking-glass with a dressing jacket thrown over her slender shoulders. Sónya stood ready dressed in the middle of the room and, pressing the head of a pin till it hurt her dainty finger, was fixing on a last ribbon that squeaked as the pin went through it.

"That's not the way, that's not the way, Sónya!" cried Natásha turning her head and clutching with both hands at her hair which the maid who was dressing it had not time to release. "That bow is not right. Come here!"

Sónya sat down and Natásha pinned the ribbon on differently.

"Allow me, Miss! I can't do it like that," said the maid who was holding Natásha's hair.

"Oh, dear! Well then, wait. That's right, Sónya."

"Aren't you ready? It is nearly ten," came the countess' voice.

"Directly! Directly! And you, Mamma?"

"I have only my cap to pin on."

"Don't do it without me!" called Natásha. "You won't do it right."

"But it's already ten."

They had decided to be at the ball by half-past ten, and Natásha had still to get dressed and they had to call at the Taurida Gardens.

When her hair was done, Natásha, in her short petticoat from under which her dancing shoes showed, and in her mother's dressing jacket, ran up to Sónya, scrutinized her, and then ran to her mother. Turning her mother's head this way and that, she fastened on the cap and, hurriedly kissing her gray hair, ran back to the maids who were turning up the hem of her skirt.

The cause of the delay was Natásha's skirt, which was too long. Two maids were turning up the hem and hurriedly biting off the ends of thread. A third with pins in her mouth was running about between the countess and Sónya, and a fourth held the whole of the gossamer garment up high on one uplifted hand.

"Mávra, quicker, darling!"

"Give me my thimble, Miss, from there..."

"Whenever will you be ready?" asked the count coming to the door. "Here is some scent. Perónskaya must be tired of waiting."

"It's ready, Miss," said the maid, holding up the shortened gauze dress with two fingers, and blowing and shaking something off it, as if by this to express a consciousness of the airiness and purity of what she held.

Natásha began putting on the dress.

"In a minute! In a minute! Don't come in, Papa!" she cried to her father as he opened the door—speaking from under the filmy skirt which still covered her whole face.

Sónya slammed the door to. A minute later they let the count in. He was wearing a blue swallow-tail coat, shoes and stockings, and was perfumed and his hair pomaded.

"Oh, Papa! how nice you look! Charming!" cried Natásha, as she stood in the middle of the room smoothing out the folds of the gauze.

"If you please, Miss! allow me," said the maid, who on her knees was pulling the skirt straight and shifting the pins from one side of her mouth to the other with her tongue.

"Say what you like," exclaimed Sónya, in a despairing voice as she looked at Natásha, "say what you like, it's still too long."

Natásha stepped back to look at herself in the pier glass. The dress *was* too long.

"Really, madam, it is not at all too long," said Mávra, crawling on her knees after her young lady.

"Well, if it's too long we'll tack it up... we'll tack it up in one minute," said the resolute Dunyásha taking a needle that was stuck on the front of her little shawl and, still kneeling on the floor, set to work once more.

At that moment, with soft steps, the countess came in shyly, in her cap and velvet gown.

"Oo-oo, my beauty!" exclaimed the count, "she looks better than any of you!"

He would have embraced her but, blushing, she stepped aside fearing to be rumpled.

"Mamma, your cap, more to this side," said Natásha. "I'll arrange it," and she rushed forward so that the maids who were tacking up her skirt could not move fast enough and a piece of gauze was torn off.

"Oh goodness! What has happened? Really it was not my fault!"

"Never mind, I'll run it up, it won't show," said Dunyásha.

"What a beauty—a very queen!" said the nurse as she came to the door. "And Sónya! They are lovely!"

At a quarter past ten they at last got into their carriages and started. But they had still to call at the Taurida Gardens.

Perónskaya was quite ready. In spite of her age and plainness she had gone through the same process as the Rostóvs, but with less flurry—for to her it was a matter of routine. Her ugly old body was washed, perfumed, and powdered in just the same way. She had washed behind her ears just as carefully, and when she entered her drawing room in her yellow dress, wearing her badge as maid of honor, her old lady's maid was as full of rapturous admiration as the Rostóvs' servants had been.

She praised the Rostóvs' toilets. They praised her taste and toilet, and at eleven o'clock, careful of their coiffures and dresses, they settled themselves in their carriages and drove off.

CHAPTER XV

Natásha had not had a moment free since early morning and had not once had time to think of what lay before her.

In the damp chill air and crowded closeness of the swaying carriage, she for the first time vividly imagined what was in store for her there at the ball, in those brightly lighted rooms—with music, flowers, dances, the Emperor, and all the brilliant young people of Petersburg. The prospect was so splendid that she hardly believed it would come true, so out of keeping was it with the chill darkness and closeness of the carriage. She understood all that awaited her only when, after stepping over the red baize at the entrance, she entered the hall, took off her fur cloak, and, besideSónya and in front of her mother, mounted the brightly illuminated stairs between the flowers. Only then did she remember how she must behave at a ball, and tried to assume the majestic air she considered indispensable for a girl on such an occasion. But, fortunately for her, she felt her eyes growing misty, she saw nothing clearly, her pulse beat a hundred to the minute, and the blood throbbed at her heart. She could not assume that pose, which would have made her ridiculous, and she moved on almost fainting from excitement and trying with all her might to conceal it. And this was the very attitude that became her best. Before and behind them other visitors were entering, also talking in low tones and wearing ball dresses. The mirrors on the landing reflected ladies in white, pale-blue, and pink dresses, with diamonds and pearls on their bare necks and arms.

Natásha looked in the mirrors and could not distinguish her reflection from the others. All was blended into one brilliant procession. On entering the ballroom the regular hum of voices, footsteps, and greetings deafened Natásha, and the light and glitter dazzled her still more. The host and hostess, who had already been standing at the door for half an hour repeating the same words to the various arrivals, *"Charmé de vousvoir,"* * greeted the Rostóvs and Perónskaya in the same manner.

* "Delighted to see you."

The two girls in their white dresses, each with a rose in her black hair, both curtsied in the same way, but the hostess' eye involuntarily rested longer on the slim Natásha. She looked at her and gave her alone a special smile in addition to her usual smile as hostess. Looking at her she may have recalled the golden, irrecoverable days of her own girlhood and her own first ball. The host also followed Natásha with his eyes and asked the count which was his daughter.

"Charming!" said he, kissing the tips of his fingers.

In the ballroom guests stood crowding at the entrance doors awaiting the Emperor. The countess took up a position in one of the front rows of that crowd. Natásha heard and felt that several people were asking about her and looking at her. She realized that those noticing her liked her, and this observation helped to calm her.

"There are some like ourselves and some worse," she thought.

Perónskaya was pointing out to the countess the most important people at the ball.

"That is the Dutch ambassador, do you see? That gray-haired man," she said, indicating an old man with a profusion of silver-gray curly hair, who was surrounded by ladies laughing at something he said.

"Ah, here she is, the Queen of Petersburg, Countess Bezúkhova," said Perónskaya, indicating Hélène who had just entered. "How lovely! She is quite equal to MáryaAntónovna. See how the men, young and old, pay court to her. Beautiful and clever... they say Prince —— is quite mad about her. But see, those two, though not good-looking, are even more run after."

She pointed to a lady who was crossing the room followed by a very plain daughter.

"She is a splendid match, a millionairess," said Perónskaya. "And look, here come her suitors."

"That is Bezúkhova's brother, Anatole Kurágin," she said, indicating a handsome officer of the Horse Guards who passed by them with head erect, looking at something over the heads of the ladies. "He's handsome, isn't he? I hear they will marry him to that rich girl. But your cousin, Drubetskóy, is also very attentive to her. They say she has millions. Oh yes, that's the French ambassador himself!" she replied to the countess' inquiry about Caulaincourt. "Looks as if he were a king! All the same, the French are charming, very charming. No one more charming in society. Ah, here she is! Yes, she is still the most beautiful of them all, our MáryaAntónovna! And how simply she is dressed! Lovely! And that stout one in spectacles is the universal Freemason," she went on, indicating Pierre. "Put him beside his wife and he looks a regular buffoon!"

Pierre, swaying his stout body, advanced, making way through the crowd and nodding to right and left as casually and good-naturedly as if he were passing through a crowd at a fair. He pushed through, evidently looking for someone.

Natásha looked joyfully at the familiar face of Pierre, "the buffoon," as Perónskaya had called him, and knew he was looking for them, and for her in particular. He had promised to be at the ball and introduce partners to her.

But before he reached them Pierre stopped beside a very handsome, dark man of middle height, and in a white uniform, who stood by a window talking to a tall man wearing stars and a ribbon. Natásha at once recognized the shorter and younger man in the white uniform: it was Bolkónski, who seemed to her to have grown much younger, happier, and better-looking.

"There's someone else we know—Bolkónski, do you see, Mamma?" said Natásha, pointing out Prince Andrew. "You remember, he stayed a night with us at Otrádnoe."

"Oh, you know him?" said Perónskaya. "I can't bear him. *Il fait à présent la pluie et le beau temps.* * He's too proud for anything. Takes after his father. And he's hand in glove with Speránski, writing some project or other. Just look how he treats the ladies! There's one talking to him and he has turned away," she said, pointing at him. "I'd give it to him if he treated me as he does those ladies."

* "He is all the rage just now."

CHAPTER XVI

Suddenly everybody stirred, began talking, and pressed forward and then back, and between the two rows, which separated, the Emperor entered to the sounds of music that had immediately struck up. Behind him walked his host and hostess. He walked in rapidly, bowing to right and left as if anxious to get the first moments of the reception over. The band played the polonaise in vogue at that time on account of the words that had been set to it, beginning: "Alexander, Elisaveta, all our hearts you ravish quite..." The Emperor passed on to the drawing room, the crowd made a rush for the doors, and several persons with excited faces hurried there and back again. Then the crowd hastily retired from the drawing room door, at which the Emperor reappeared talking to the hostess. A young man, looking distraught, pounced down on the ladies, asking them to move aside. Some ladies, with faces betraying complete forgetfulness of all the rules of decorum, pushed forward to the detriment of their toilets. The men began to choose partners and take their places for the polonaise.

Everyone moved back, and the Emperor came smiling out of the drawing room leading his hostess by the hand but not keeping time to the music. The host followed with MáryaAntónovnaNarýshkina; then came ambassadors, ministers, and various generals, whom Perónskaya diligently named. More than half the ladies already had partners and were taking up, or preparing to take up, their positions for the polonaise. Natásha felt that she would be left with her mother and Sónya among a minority of women who crowded near the wall, not having been invited to dance. She stood with her slender arms hanging down, her scarcely defined bosom rising and falling regularly, and with bated breath and glittering, frightened eyes gazed straight before her, evidently prepared for the height of joy or misery. She was not concerned about the Emperor or any of those great people whom Perónskaya was pointing out—she had but one thought: "Is it possible no one will ask me, that I shall not be among the first to dance? Is it possible that not one of all these men will notice me? They do not even seem to see me, or if they do they look as if they were saying, 'Ah, she's not the one I'm after, so it's not worth looking at her!' No, it's impossible," she thought. "They must know how I long to dance, how splendidly I dance, and how they would enjoy dancing with me."

The strains of the polonaise, which had continued for a considerable time, had begun to sound like a sad reminiscence to Natásha's ears. She wanted to cry. Perónskaya had left them. The count was at the other end of the room. She and the countess and Sónya were standing by themselves as in the depths of a forest amid that crowd of strangers, with no one interested in them and not wanted by anyone. Prince Andrew with a lady passed by, evidently not recognizing them. The handsome Anatole was smilingly talking to a partner on his arm and looked at Natásha as one looks at a wall. Borís passed them twice and each time turned away. Berg and his wife, who were not dancing, came up to them.

This family gathering seemed humiliating to Natásha—as if there were nowhere else for the family to talk but here at the ball. She did not listen to or look at Véra, who was telling her something about her own green dress.

At last the Emperor stopped beside his last partner (he had danced with three) and the music ceased. A worried aide-de-camp ran up to the Rostóvs requesting them to stand farther back, though as it was they were already close to the wall, and from the gallery resounded the distinct, precise, enticingly rhythmical strains of a waltz. The Emperor looked smilingly down the room. A minute passed but no one had yet begun dancing. An aide-de-camp, the Master of Ceremonies, went up to Countess Bezúkhova and asked her to dance. She smilingly raised her hand and laid it on his shoulder without looking at him. The aide-de-camp, an adept in his art, grasping his partner firmly round her waist, with confident deliberation started smoothly, gliding first round the edge of the circle, then at the corner of the room he caught Hélène's left hand and turned her, the only sound audible, apart from the ever-quickening music, being the rhythmic click of the spurs on his rapid, agile feet, while at every third beat his partner's velvet dress spread out and seemed to flash as she whirled round. Natásha gazed at them and was ready to cry because it was not she who was dancing that first turn of the waltz.

Prince Andrew, in the white uniform of a cavalry colonel, wearing stockings and dancing shoes, stood looking animated and bright in the front row of the circle not far from the Rostóvs. Baron Firhoff was talking to him about the first sitting of the Council of State to be held next day. Prince Andrew, as one closely connected with Speránski and participating in the work of the legislative commission, could give reliable information about that sitting, concerning which various rumors were current. But not listening to what Firhoff was saying, he was gazing now at the sovereign and now at the men intending to dance who had not yet gathered courage to enter the circle.

Prince Andrew was watching these men abashed by the Emperor's presence, and the women who were breathlessly longing to be asked to dance.

Pierre came up to him and caught him by the arm.

"You always dance. I have a protégée, the young Rostóva, here. Ask her," he said.

"Where is she?" asked Bolkónski. "Excuse me!" he added, turning to the baron, "we will finish this conversation elsewhere—at a ball one must dance." He stepped forward in the direction Pierre indicated. The despairing, dejected expression of Natásha's face caught his eye. He recognized her, guessed her feelings, saw that it was her début, remembered her conversation at the window, and with an expression of pleasure on his face approached Countess Rostóva.

"Allow me to introduce you to my daughter," said the countess, with heightened color.

"I have the pleasure of being already acquainted, if the countess remembers me," said Prince Andrew with a low and courteous bow quite belying Perónskaya's remarks about his rudeness, and approaching Natásha he held out his arm to grasp her waist before he had completed his invitation. He asked her to waltz. That tremulous expression on Natásha's face, prepared either for despair or rapture, suddenly brightened into a happy, grateful, childlike smile.

"I have long been waiting for you," that frightened happy little girl seemed to say by the smile that replaced the threatened tears, as she raised her hand to Prince Andrew's shoulder. They were the second couple to enter the circle. Prince Andrew was one of the best dancers of his day and Natásha danced exquisitely. Her little feet in their white satin dancing shoes did their work swiftly, lightly, and independently of herself, while her face beamed with ecstatic happiness. Her slender bare arms and neck were not beautiful—compared to Hélène's her shoulders looked thin and her bosom undeveloped. But Hélène seemed, as it were, hardened by a varnish left by the thousands of looks that had scanned her person, while Natásha was like a girl exposed for the first time, who would have felt very much ashamed had she not been assured that this was absolutely necessary.

Prince Andrew liked dancing, and wishing to escape as quickly as possible from the political and clever talk which everyone addressed to him, wishing also to break up the circle of restraint he disliked, caused by the Emperor's presence, he danced, and had chosen Natásha because Pierre pointed her out to him and because she was the first pretty girl who caught his eye; but scarcely had he embraced that slender supple figure and felt her stirring so close to him and smiling so near him than the wine of her charm rose to his head, and he felt himself revived and rejuvenated when after leaving her he stood breathing deeply and watching the other dancers.

CHAPTER XVII

After Prince Andrew, Borís came up to ask Natásha for a dance, and then the aide-de-camp who had opened the ball, and several other young men, so that, flushed and happy, and passing on her superfluous partners to Sónya, she did not cease dancing all the evening. She noticed and saw nothing of what occupied everyone else. Not only did she fail to notice that the Emperor talked a long time with the French ambassador, and how particularly gracious he was to a certain lady, or that Prince So-and-so and So-and-so did and said this and that, and that Hélène had great success and was honored by the special attention of So-and-so, but she did not even see the Emperor, and only noticed that he had gone because the ball became livelier after his departure. For one of the merry cotillions before supper Prince Andrew was again her partner. He reminded her of their first encounter in the Otrádnoe avenue, and how she had been unable to sleep that moonlight night, and told her how he had involuntarily overheard her. Natásha blushed at that recollection and tried to excuse herself, as if there had been something to be ashamed of in what Prince Andrew had overheard.

Like all men who have grown up in society, Prince Andrew liked meeting someone there not of the conventional society stamp. And such was Natásha, with her surprise, her delight, her shyness, and even her mistakes in speaking French. With her he behaved with special care and tenderness, sitting beside her and talking of the simplest and most unimportant matters; he admired her shy grace.

In the middle of the cotillion, having completed one of the figures, Natásha, still out of breath, was returning to her seat when another dancer chose her. She was tired and panting and evidently thought of declining, but immediately put her hand gaily on the man's shoulder, smiling at Prince Andrew.

"I'd be glad to sit beside you and rest: I'm tired; but you see how they keep asking me, and I'm glad of it, I'm happy and I love everybody, and you and I understand it all," and much, much more was said in her smile. When her partner left her Natásha ran across the room to choose two ladies for the figure.

"If she goes to her cousin first and then to another lady, she will be my wife," said Prince Andrew to himself quite to his own surprise, as he watched her. She did go first to her cousin.

"What rubbish sometimes enters one's head!" thought Prince Andrew, "but what is certain is that that girl is so charming, so original, that she won't be dancing here a month before she will be married.... Such as she are rare here," he thought, as Natásha, readjusting a rose that was slipping on her bodice, settled herself beside him.

When the cotillion was over the old count in his blue coat came up to the dancers. He invited Prince Andrew to come and see them, and asked his daughter whether she was enjoying herself. Natásha did not answer at once but only looked up with a smile that said reproachfully: "How can you ask such a question?"

"I have never enjoyed myself so much before!" she said, and Prince Andrew noticed how her thin arms rose quickly as if to embrace her father and instantly dropped again. Natásha was happier than she had ever been in her life. She was at that height of bliss when one becomes completely kind and good and does not believe in the possibility of evil, unhappiness, or sorrow.

At that ball Pierre for the first time felt humiliated by the position his wife occupied in court circles. He was gloomy and absent-minded. A deep furrow ran across his forehead, and standing by a window he stared over his spectacles seeing no one.

On her way to supper Natásha passed him.

Pierre's gloomy, unhappy look struck her. She stopped in front of him. She wished to help him, to bestow on him the superabundance of her own happiness.

"How delightful it is, Count!" said she. "Isn't it?"

Pierre smiled absent-mindedly, evidently not grasping what she said.

"Yes, I am very glad," he said.

"How can people be dissatisfied with anything?" thought Natásha. "Especially such a capital fellow as Bezúkhov!" In Natásha's eyes all the people at the ball alike were good, kind, and splendid people, loving one another; none of them capable of injuring another—and so they ought all to be happy.

CHAPTER XVIII

Next day Prince Andrew thought of the ball, but his mind did not dwell on it long. "Yes, it was a very brilliant ball," and then... "Yes, that little Rostóva is very charming. There's something fresh, original, un-Petersburg-like about her that distinguishes her." That was all he thought about yesterday's ball, and after his morning tea he set to work.

But either from fatigue or want of sleep he was ill-disposed for work and could get nothing done. He kept criticizing his own work, as he often did, and was glad when he heard someone coming.

The visitor was Bítski, who served on various committees, frequented all the societies in Petersburg, and was a passionate devotee of the new ideas and of Speránski, and a diligent Petersburg newsmonger—one of those men who choose their opinions like their clothes according to the fashion, but who for that very reason appear to be the warmest partisans. Hardly had he got rid of his hat before he ran into Prince Andrew's room with a preoccupied air and at once began talking. He had just heard particulars of that morning's sitting of the Council of State opened by the Emperor, and he spoke of it enthusiastically. The Emperor's speech had been extraordinary. It had been a speech such as only constitutional monarchs deliver. "The Sovereign plainly said that the Council and Senate are *estates* of the realm, he said that the government must rest not on authority but on secure bases. The Emperor said that the fiscal system must be reorganized and the accounts published," recounted Bítski, emphasizing certain words and opening his eyes significantly.

"Ah, yes! Today's events mark an epoch, the greatest epoch in our history," he concluded.

Prince Andrew listened to the account of the opening of the Council of State, which he had so impatiently awaited and to which he had attached such importance, and was surprised that this event, now that it had taken place, did not affect him, and even seemed quite insignificant. He listened with quiet irony to Bítski's enthusiastic account of it. A very simple thought occurred to him: "What does it matter to me or to Bítski what the Emperor was pleased to say at the Council? Can all that make me any happier or better?"

And this simple reflection suddenly destroyed all the interest Prince Andrew had felt in the impending reforms. He was going to dine that evening at Speránski's, "with only a few friends," as the host had said when inviting him. The prospect of that dinner in the intimate home circle of the man he so admired had greatly interested Prince Andrew, especially as he had not yet seen Speránski in his domestic surroundings, but now he felt disinclined to go to it.

At the appointed hour, however, he entered the modest house Speránski owned in the Taurida Gardens. In the parqueted dining room of this small house, remarkable for its extreme cleanliness (suggesting that of a monastery), Prince Andrew, who was rather late, found the friendly gathering of Speránski's intimate acquaintances already assembled at five o'clock. There were no ladies present except Speránski's little daughter (long-faced like her father) and her governess. The other guests were Gervais, Magnítski, and Stolýpin. While still in the anteroom Prince Andrew heard loud voices and a ringing staccato laugh—a laugh such as one hears on the stage. Someone—it sounded like Speránski—was distinctly ejaculating *ha-ha-ha*. Prince Andrew had never before heard Speránski's famous laugh, and this ringing, high-pitched laughter from a statesman made a strange impression on him.

He entered the dining room. The whole company were standing between two windows at a small table laid with hors-d'oeuvres. Speránski, wearing a gray swallow-tail coat with a star on the breast, and evidently still the same waistcoat and high white stock he had worn at the meeting of the Council of State, stood at the table with a beaming countenance. His guests surrounded him. Magnítski, addressing himself to Speránski, was relating an anecdote, and Speránski was laughing in advance at what Magnítski was going to say. When Prince Andrew entered the room Magnítski's words were again crowned by laughter. Stolýpin gave a deep bass guffaw as he munched a piece of bread and cheese. Gervais laughed softly with a hissing chuckle, and Speránski in a high-pitched staccato manner.

Still laughing, Speránski held out his soft white hand to Prince Andrew.

"Very pleased to see you, Prince," he said. "One moment..." he went on, turning to Magnítski and interrupting his story. "We have agreed that this is a dinner for recreation, with not a word about business!" and turning again to the narrator he began to laugh afresh.

Prince Andrew looked at the laughing Speránski with astonishment, regret, and disillusionment. It seemed to him that this was not Speránski but someone else. Everything that had formerly appeared mysterious and fascinating in Speránski suddenly became plain and unattractive.

At dinner the conversation did not cease for a moment and seemed to consist of the contents of a book of funny anecdotes. Before Magnítski had finished his story someone else was anxious to relate something still funnier. Most of the anecdotes, if not relating to the state service, related to people in the service. It seemed that in this company the insignificance of those people was so definitely accepted that the only possible attitude toward them was one of good humored ridicule. Speránski related how at the Council that morning a deaf dignitary, when asked his opinion, replied that he thought so too. Gervais gave a long account of an official revision, remarkable for the stupidity of everybody concerned. Stolýpin, stuttering, broke into the conversation and began excitedly talking of the abuses that existed under the former order of things—threatening to give a serious turn to the conversation. Magnítski starting quizzing Stolýpin about his vehemence. Gervais intervened with a joke, and the talk reverted to its former lively tone.

Evidently Speránski liked to rest after his labors and find amusement in a circle of friends, and his guests, understanding his wish, tried to enliven him and amuse themselves. But their gaiety seemed to Prince Andrew mirthless and tiresome. Speránski's high-pitched voice struck him unpleasantly, and the incessant laughter grated on him like a false note. Prince Andrew did not laugh and feared that he would be a damper on the spirits of the company, but no one took any notice of his being out of harmony with the general mood. They all seemed very gay.

He tried several times to join in the conversation, but his remarks were tossed aside each time like a cork thrown out of the water, and he could not jest with them.

There was nothing wrong or unseemly in what they said, it was witty and might have been funny, but it lacked just that something which is the salt of mirth, and they were not even aware that such a thing existed.

After dinner Speránski's daughter and her governess rose. He patted the little girl with his white hand and kissed her. And that gesture, too, seemed unnatural to Prince Andrew.

The men remained at table over their port—English fashion. In the midst of a conversation that was started about Napoleon's Spanish affairs, which they all agreed in approving, Prince Andrew began to express a contrary opinion. Speránski smiled and, with an evident wish to prevent the conversation from taking an unpleasant course, told a story that had no connection with the previous conversation. For a few moments all were silent.

Having sat some time at table, Speránski corked a bottle of wine and, remarking, "Nowadays good wine rides in a carriage and pair," passed it to the servant and got up. All rose and continuing to talk loudly went into the drawing room. Two letters brought by a courier were handed to Speránski and he took them to his study. As soon as he had left the room the general merriment stopped and the guests began to converse sensibly and quietly with one another.

"Now for the recitation!" said Speránski on returning from his study. "A wonderful talent!" he said to Prince Andrew, and Magnítski immediately assumed a pose and began reciting some humorous verses in French which he had composed about various well-known Petersburg people. He was interrupted several times by applause. When the verses were finished Prince Andrew went up to Speránski and took his leave.

"Where are you off to so early?" asked Speránski.

"I promised to go to a reception."

They said no more. Prince Andrew looked closely into those mirrorlike, impenetrable eyes, and felt that it had been ridiculous of him to have expected anything from Speránski and from any of his own activities connected with him, or ever to have attributed importance to what Speránski was doing. That precise, mirthless laughter rang in Prince Andrew's ears long after he had left the house.

When he reached home Prince Andrew began thinking of his life in Petersburg during those last four months as if it were something new. He recalled his exertions and solicitations, and the history of his project of army reform, which had been accepted for consideration and which they were trying to pass over in silence simply because another, a very poor one, had already been prepared and submitted to the Emperor. He thought of the meetings of a committee of which Berg was a member. He remembered how carefully and at what length everything relating to form and procedure was discussed at those meetings, and how sedulously and promptly all that related to the gist of the business was evaded. He recalled his labors on the Legal Code, and how painstakingly he had translated the articles of the Roman and French codes into Russian, and he felt ashamed of himself. Then he vividly pictured to himself Boguchárovo, his occupations in the country, his journey to Ryazán; he remembered the peasants and Dron the village elder, and mentally applying to them the Personal Rights he had divided into paragraphs, he felt astonished that he could have spent so much time on such useless work.

CHAPTER XIX

Next day Prince Andrew called at a few houses he had not visited before, and among them at the Rostóvs' with whom he had renewed acquaintance at the ball. Apart from considerations of politeness which demanded the call, he wanted to see that original, eager girl who had left such a pleasant impression on his mind, in her own home.

Natásha was one of the first to meet him. She was wearing a dark-blue house dress in which Prince Andrew thought her even prettier than in her ball dress. She and all the Rostóv family welcomed him as an old friend, simply and cordially. The whole family, whom he had formerly judged severely, now seemed to him to consist of excellent, simple, and kindly people. The old count's hospitality and good nature, which struck one especially in Petersburg as a pleasant surprise, were such that Prince Andrew could not refuse to stay to dinner. "Yes," he thought, "they are capital people, who of course have not the slightest idea what a treasure they possess in Natásha; but they are kindly folk and form the best possible setting for this strikingly poetic, charming girl, overflowing with life!"

In Natásha Prince Andrew was conscious of a strange world completely alien to him and brimful of joys unknown to him, a different world, that in the Otrádnoe avenue and at the window that moonlight night had already begun to disconcert him. Now this world disconcerted him no longer and was no longer alien to him, but he himself having entered it found in it a new enjoyment.

After dinner Natásha, at Prince Andrew's request, went to the clavichord and began singing. Prince Andrew stood by a window talking to the ladies and listened to her. In the midst of a phrase he ceased speaking and suddenly felt tears choking him, a thing he had thought impossible for him. He looked at Natásha as she sang, and something new and joyful stirred in his soul. He felt happy and at the same time sad. He had absolutely nothing to weep about yet he was ready to weep. What about? His former love? The little princess? His disillusionments?... His hopes for the future?... Yes and no. The chief reason was a sudden, vivid sense of the terrible contrast between something infinitely great and illimitable within him and that limited and material something that he, and even she, was. This contrast weighed on and yet cheered him while she sang.

As soon as Natásha had finished she went up to him and asked how he liked her voice. She asked this and then became confused, feeling that she ought not to have asked it. He smiled, looking at her, and said he liked her singing as he liked everything she did.

Prince Andrew left the Rostóvs' late in the evening. He went to bed from habit, but soon realized that he could not sleep. Having lit his candle he sat up in bed, then got up, then lay down again not at all troubled by his sleeplessness: his soul was as fresh and joyful as if he had stepped out of a stuffy room into God's own fresh air. It did not enter his head that he was in love with Natásha; he was not thinking about her, but only picturing her to himself, and in consequence all life appeared in a new light. "Why do I strive, why do I toil in this narrow, confined frame, when life, all life with all its joys, is open to me?" said he to himself. And for the first time for a very long while he began making happy plans for the future. He decided that he must attend to his son's education by finding a tutor and putting the boy in his charge, then he ought to retire from the service and go abroad, and see England, Switzerland and Italy. "I must use my freedom while I feel so much strength and youth in me," he said to himself. "Pierre was right when he said one must believe in the possibility of happiness in order to be happy, and now I do believe in it. Let the dead bury their dead, but while one has life one must live and be happy!" thought he.

CHAPTER XX

One morning Colonel Berg, whom Pierre knew as he knew everybody in Moscow and Petersburg, came to see him. Berg arrived in an immaculate brand-new uniform, with his hair pomaded and brushed forward over his temples as the Emperor Alexander wore his hair.

"I have just been to see the countess, your wife. Unfortunately she could not grant my request, but I hope, Count, I shall be more fortunate with you," he said with a smile.

"What is it you wish, Colonel? I am at your service."

"I have now quite settled in my new rooms, Count" (Berg said this with perfect conviction that this information could not but be agreeable), "and so I wish to arrange just a small party for my own and my wife's friends." (He smiled still more pleasantly.) "I wished to ask the countess and you to do me the honor of coming to tea and to supper."

Only Countess Hélène, considering the society of such people as the Bergs beneath her, could be cruel enough to refuse such an invitation. Berg explained so clearly why he wanted to collect at his house a small but select company, and why this would give him pleasure, and why though he grudged spending money on cards or anything harmful, he was prepared to run into some expense for the sake of good society—that Pierre could not refuse, and promised to come.

"But don't be late, Count, if I may venture to ask; about ten minutes to eight, please. We shall make up a rubber. Our general is coming. He is very good to me. We shall have supper, Count. So you will do me the favor."

Contrary to his habit of being late, Pierre on that day arrived at the Bergs' house, not at ten but at fifteen minutes to eight.

Having prepared everything necessary for the party, the Bergs were ready for their guests' arrival.

In their new, clean, and light study with its small busts and pictures and new furniture sat Berg and his wife. Berg, closely buttoned up in his new uniform, sat beside his wife explaining to her that one always could and should be acquainted with people above one, because only then does one get satisfaction from acquaintances.

"You can get to know something, you can ask for something. See how I managed from my first promotion." (Berg measured his life not by years but by promotions.) "My comrades are still nobodies, while I am only waiting for a vacancy to command a regiment, and have the happiness to be your husband." (He rose and kissed Véra's hand, and on the way to her straightened out a turned-up corner of the carpet.) "And how have I obtained all this? Chiefly by knowing how to choose my aquaintances. It goes without saying that one must be conscientious and methodical."

Berg smiled with a sense of his superiority over a weak woman, and paused, reflecting that this dear wife of his was after all but a weak woman who could not understand all that constitutes a man's dignity, what it was *ein Mann zu sein.* * Véra at the same time smiling with a sense of superiority over her good, conscientious husband, who all the same understood life wrongly, as according to Véra all men did. Berg, judging by his wife, thought all women weak and foolish. Véra, judging only by her husband and generalizing from that observation, supposed that all men, though they understand nothing and are conceited and selfish, ascribe common sense to themselves alone.

* To be a man.

Berg rose and embraced his wife carefully, so as not to crush her lace fichu for which he had paid a good price, kissing her straight on the lips.

"The only thing is, we mustn't have children too soon," he continued, following an unconscious sequence of ideas.

"Yes," answered Véra, "I don't at all want that. We must live for society."

"Princess Yusúpova wore one exactly like this," said Berg, pointing to the fichu with a happy and kindly smile.

Just then Count Bezúkhov was announced. Husband and wife glanced at one another, both smiling with self-satisfaction, and each mentally claiming the honor of this visit.

"This is what comes of knowing how to make acquaintances," thought Berg. "This is what comes of knowing how to conduct oneself."

"But please don't interrupt me when I am entertaining the guests," said Véra, "because I know what interests each of them and what to say to different people."

Berg smiled again.

"It can't be helped: men must sometimes have masculine conversation," said he.

They received Pierre in their small, new drawing room, where it was impossible to sit down anywhere without disturbing its symmetry, neatness, and order; so it was quite comprehensible and not strange that Berg, having generously offered to disturb the symmetry of an armchair or of the sofa for his dear guest, but being apparently painfully undecided on the matter himself, eventually left the visitor to settle the question of selection. Pierre disturbed the symmetry by moving a chair for himself, and Berg and Véra immediately began their evening party, interrupting each other in their efforts to entertain their guest.

Véra, having decided in her own mind that Pierre ought to be entertained with conversation about the French embassy, at once began accordingly. Berg, having decided that masculine conversation was required, interrupted his wife's remarks and touched on the question of the war with Austria, and unconsciously jumped from the general subject to personal considerations as to the proposals made him to take part in the Austrian campaign and the reasons why he had declined them. Though the conversation was very incoherent and Véra was angry at the intrusion of the masculine element, both husband and wife felt with satisfaction that, even if only one guest was present, their evening had begun very well and was as like as two peas to every other evening party with its talk, tea, and lighted candles.

Before long Borís, Berg's old comrade, arrived. There was a shade of condescension and patronage in his treatment of Berg and Véra. After Borís came a lady with the colonel, then the general himself, then the Rostóvs, and the party became unquestionably exactly like all other evening parties. Berg and Véra could not repress their smiles of satisfaction at the sight of all this movement in their drawing room, at the sound of the disconnected talk, the rustling of dresses, and the bowing and scraping. Everything was just as everybody always has it, especially so the general, who admired the apartment, patted Berg on the shoulder, and with parental authority superintended the setting out of the table for boston. The general sat down by Count IlyáRostóv, who was next to himself the most important guest. The old people sat with the old, the young with the young, and the hostess at the tea table, on which stood exactly the same kind of cakes in a silver cake basket as the Panins had at their party. Everything was just as it was everywhere else.

CHAPTER XXI

Pierre, as one of the principal guests, had to sit down to boston with Count Rostóv, the general, and the colonel. At the card table he happened to be directly facing Natásha, and was struck by a curious change that had come over her since the ball. She was silent, and not only less pretty than at the ball, but only redeemed from plainness by her look of gentle indifference to everything around.

"What's the matter with her?" thought Pierre, glancing at her. She was sitting by her sister at the tea table, and reluctantly, without looking at him, made some reply to Borís who sat down beside her. After playing out a whole suit and to his partner's delight taking five tricks, Pierre, hearing greetings and the steps of someone who had entered the room while he was picking up his tricks, glanced again at Natásha.

"What has happened to her?" he asked himself with still greater surprise.

Prince Andrew was standing before her, saying something to her with a look of tender solicitude. She, having raised her head, was looking up at him, flushed and evidently trying to master her rapid breathing. And the bright glow of some inner fire that had been suppressed was again alight in her. She was completely transformed and from a plain girl had again become what she had been at the ball.

Prince Andrew went up to Pierre, and the latter noticed a new and youthful expression in his friend's face.

Pierre changed places several times during the game, sitting now with his back to Natásha and now facing her, but during the whole of the six rubbers he watched her and his friend.

"Something very important is happening between them," thought Pierre, and a feeling that was both joyful and painful agitated him and made him neglect the game.

After six rubbers the general got up, saying that it was no use playing like that, and Pierre was released. Natásha on one side was talking with Sónya and Borís, and Véra with a subtle smile was saying something to Prince Andrew. Pierre went up to his friend and, asking whether they were talking secrets, sat down beside them. Véra, having noticed Prince Andrew's attentions to Natásha, decided that at a party, a real evening party, subtle allusions to the tender passion were absolutely necessary and, seizing a moment when Prince Andrew was alone, began a conversation with him about feelings in general and about her sister. With so intellectual a guest as she considered Prince Andrew to be, she felt that she had to employ her diplomatic tact.

When Pierre went up to them he noticed that Véra was being carried away by her self-satisfied talk, but that Prince Andrew seemed embarrassed, a thing that rarely happened with him.

"What do you think?" Véra was saying with an arch smile. "You are so discerning, Prince, and understand people's characters so well at a glance. What do you think of Natalie? Could she be constant in her attachments? Could she, like other women" (Véra meant herself), "love a man once for all and remain true to him forever? That is what I consider true love. What do you think, Prince?"

"I know your sister too little," replied Prince Andrew, with a sarcastic smile under which he wished to hide his embarrassment, "to be able to solve so delicate a question, and then I have noticed that the less attractive a woman is the more constant she is likely to be," he added, and looked up at Pierre who was just approaching them.

"Yes, that is true, Prince. In our days," continued Véra—mentioning "our days" as people of limited intelligence are fond of doing, imagining that they have discovered and appraised the peculiarities of "our days" and that human characteristics change with the times—"in our days a girl has so much freedom that the pleasure of being courted often stifles real feeling in her. And it must be confessed that Natalie is very susceptible." This return to the subject of Natalie caused Prince Andrew to knit his brows with discomfort: he was about to rise, but Véra continued with a still more subtle smile:

"I think no one has been more courted than she," she went on, "but till quite lately she never cared seriously for anyone. Now you know, Count," she said to Pierre, "even our dear cousin Borís, who, between ourselves, was very far gone in the land of tenderness..." (alluding to a map of love much in vogue at that time).

Prince Andrew frowned and remained silent.

"You are friendly with Borís, aren't you?" asked Véra.

"Yes, I know him...."

"I expect he has told you of his childish love for Natásha?"

"Oh, there was childish love?" suddenly asked Prince Andrew, blushing unexpectedly.

"Yes, you know between cousins intimacy often leads to love. *Le cousinage est un dangereuxvoisinage.* * Don't you think so?"

* "Cousinhood is a dangerous neighborhood."

"Oh, undoubtedly!" said Prince Andrew, and with sudden and unnatural liveliness he began chaffing Pierre about the need to be very careful with his fifty-year-old Moscow cousins, and in the midst of these jesting remarks he rose, taking Pierre by the arm, and drew him aside.

"Well?" asked Pierre, seeing his friend's strange animation with surprise, and noticing the glance he turned on Natásha as he rose.

"I must... I must have a talk with you," said Prince Andrew. "You know that pair of women's gloves?" (He referred to the Masonic gloves given to a newly initiated Brother to present to the woman he loved.) "I... but no, I will talk to you later on," and with a strange light in his eyes and restlessness in his movements, Prince Andrew approached Natásha and sat down beside her. Pierre saw how Prince Andrew asked her something and how she flushed as she replied.

But at that moment Berg came to Pierre and began insisting that he should take part in an argument between the general and the colonel on the affairs in Spain.

Berg was satisfied and happy. The smile of pleasure never left his face. The party was very successful and quite like other parties he had seen. Everything was similar: the ladies' subtle talk, the cards, the general raising his voice at the card table, and the samovar and the tea cakes; only one thing was lacking that he had always seen at the evening parties he wished to imitate. They had not yet had a loud conversation among the men and a dispute about something important and clever. Now the general had begun such a discussion and so Berg drew Pierre to it.

CHAPTER XXII

Next day, having been invited by the count, Prince Andrew dined with the Rostóvs and spent the rest of the day there.

Everyone in the house realized for whose sake Prince Andrew came, and without concealing it he tried to be with Natásha all day. Not only in the soul of the frightened yet happy and enraptured Natásha, but in the whole house, there was a feeling of awe at something important that was bound to happen. The countess looked with sad and sternly serious eyes at Prince Andrew when he talked to Natásha and timidly started some artificial conversation about trifles as soon as he looked her way. Sónya was afraid to leave Natásha and afraid of being in the way when she was with them. Natásha grew pale, in a panic of expectation, when she remained alone with him for a moment. Prince Andrew surprised her by his timidity. She felt that he wanted to say something to her but could not bring himself to do so.

In the evening, when Prince Andrew had left, the countess went up to Natásha and whispered: "Well, what?"

"Mamma! For heaven's sake don't ask me anything now! One can't talk about that," said Natásha.

But all the same that night Natásha, now agitated and now frightened, lay a long time in her mother's bed gazing straight before her. She told her how he had complimented her, how he told her he was going abroad, asked her where they were going to spend the summer, and then how he had asked her about Borís.

"But such a... such a... never happened to me before!" she said. "Only I feel afraid in his presence. I am always afraid when I'm with him. What does that mean? Does it mean that it's the real thing? Yes? Mamma, are you asleep?"

"No, my love; I am frightened myself," answered her mother. "Now go!"

"All the same I shan't sleep. What silliness, to sleep! Mummy! Mummy! such a thing never happened to me before," she said, surprised and alarmed at the feeling she was aware of in herself. "And could we ever have thought!..."

It seemed to Natásha that even at the time she first saw Prince Andrew at Otrádnoe she had fallen in love with him. It was as if she feared this strange, unexpected happiness of meeting again the very man she had then chosen (she was firmly convinced she had done so) and of finding him, as it seemed, not indifferent to her.

"And it had to happen that he should come specially to Petersburg while we are here. And it had to happen that we should meet at that ball. It is fate. Clearly it is fate that everything led up to this! Already *then*, directly I saw him I felt something peculiar."

"What else did he say to you? What are those verses? Read them..." said her mother, thoughtfully, referring to some verses Prince Andrew had written in Natásha's album.

"Mamma, one need not be ashamed of his being a widower?"

"Don't, Natásha! Pray to God. 'Marriages are made in heaven,'" said her mother.

"Darling Mummy, how I love you! How happy I am!" cried Natásha, shedding tears of joy and excitement and embracing her mother.

At that very time Prince Andrew was sitting with Pierre and telling him of his love for Natásha and his firm resolve to make her his wife.

That day Countess Hélène had a reception at her house. The French ambassador was there, and a foreign prince of the blood who had of late become a frequent visitor of hers, and many brilliant ladies and gentlemen. Pierre, who had come downstairs, walked through the rooms and struck everyone by his preoccupied, absent-minded, and morose air.

Since the ball he had felt the approach of a fit of nervous depression and had made desperate efforts to combat it. Since the intimacy of his wife with the royal prince, Pierre had unexpectedly been made a gentleman of the bedchamber, and from that time he had begun to feel oppressed and ashamed in court society, and dark thoughts of the vanity of all things human came to him oftener than before. At the same time the feeling he had noticed between his protégée Natásha and Prince Andrew accentuated his gloom by the contrast between his own position and his friend's. He tried equally to avoid thinking about his wife, and about Natásha and Prince Andrew; and again everything seemed to him insignificant in comparison with eternity; again the question: for what? presented itself; and he forced himself to work day and night at Masonic labors, hoping to drive away the evil spirit that threatened him. Toward midnight, after he had left the countess' apartments, he was sitting upstairs in a shabby dressing gown, copying out the original transaction of the Scottish lodge of Freemasons at a table in his low room cloudy with tobacco smoke, when someone came in. It was Prince Andrew.

"Ah, it's you!" said Pierre with a preoccupied, dissatisfied air. "And I, you see, am hard at it." He pointed to his manuscript book with that air of escaping from the ills of life with which unhappy people look at their work.

Prince Andrew, with a beaming, ecstatic expression of renewed life on his face, paused in front of Pierre and, not noticing his sad look, smiled at him with the egotism of joy.

"Well, dear heart," said he, "I wanted to tell you about it yesterday and I have come to do so today. I never experienced anything like it before. I am in love, my friend!"

Suddenly Pierre heaved a deep sigh and dumped his heavy person down on the sofa beside Prince Andrew.

"With NatáshaRostóva, yes?" said he.

"Yes, yes! Who else should it be? I should never have believed it, but the feeling is stronger than I. Yesterday I tormented myself and suffered, but I would not exchange even that torment for anything in the world, I have not lived till now. At last I live, but I can't live without her! But can she love me?... I am too old for her.... Why don't you speak?"

"I? I? What did I tell you?" said Pierre suddenly, rising and beginning to pace up and down the room. "I always thought it.... That girl is such a treasure... she is a rare girl.... My dear friend, I entreat you, don't philosophize, don't doubt, marry, marry, marry.... And I am sure there will not be a happier man than you."

"But what of her?"

"She loves you."

"Don't talk rubbish..." said Prince Andrew, smiling and looking into Pierre's eyes.

"She does, I know," Pierre cried fiercely.

"But do listen," returned Prince Andrew, holding him by the arm. "Do you know the condition I am in? I must talk about it to someone."

"Well, go on, go on. I am very glad," said Pierre, and his face really changed, his brow became smooth, and he listened gladly to Prince Andrew. Prince Andrew seemed, and really was, quite a different, quite a new man. Where was his spleen, his contempt for life, his disillusionment? Pierre was the only person to whom he made up his mind to speak openly; and to him he told all that was in his soul. Now he boldly and lightly made plans for an extended future, said he could not sacrifice his own happiness to his father's caprice, and spoke of how he would either make his father consent to this marriage and love her, or would do without his consent; then he marveled at the feeling that had mastered him as at something strange, apart from and independent of himself.

"I should not have believed anyone who told me that I was capable of such love," said Prince Andrew. "It is not at all the same feeling that I knew in the past. The whole world is now for me divided into two halves: one half is she, and there all is joy, hope, light: the other half is everything where she is not, and there is all gloom and darkness...."

"Darkness and gloom," reiterated Pierre: "yes, yes, I understand that."

"I cannot help loving the light, it is not my fault. And I am very happy! You understand me? I know you are glad for my sake."

"Yes, yes," Pierre assented, looking at his friend with a touched and sad expression in his eyes. The brighter Prince Andrew's lot appeared to him, the gloomier seemed his own.

CHAPTER XXIII

Prince Andrew needed his father's consent to his marriage, and to obtain this he started for the country next day.

His father received his son's communication with external composure, but inward wrath. He could not comprehend how anyone could wish to alter his life or introduce anything new into it, when his own life was already ending. "If only they would let me end my days as I want to," thought the old man, "then they might do as they please." With his son, however, he employed the diplomacy he reserved for important occasions and, adopting a quiet tone, discussed the whole matter.

In the first place the marriage was not a brilliant one as regards birth, wealth, or rank. Secondly, Prince Andrew was no longer as young as he had been and his health was poor (the old man laid special stress on this), while she was very young. Thirdly, he had a son whom it would be a pity to entrust to a chit of a girl. "Fourthly and finally," the father said, looking ironically at his son, "I beg you to put it off for a year: go abroad, take a cure, look out as you wanted to for a German tutor for Prince Nicholas. Then if your love or passion or obstinacy—as you please—is still as great, marry! And that's my last word on it. Mind, the last..." concluded the prince, in a tone which showed that nothing would make him alter his decision.

Prince Andrew saw clearly that the old man hoped that his feelings, or his fiancée's, would not stand a year's test, or that he (the old prince himself) would die before then, and he decided to conform to his father's wish—to propose, and postpone the wedding for a year.

Three weeks after the last evening he had spent with the Rostóvs, Prince Andrew returned to Petersburg.

Next day after her talk with her mother Natásha expected Bolkónski all day, but he did not come. On the second and third day it was the same. Pierre did not come either and Natásha, not knowing that Prince Andrew had gone to see his father, could not explain his absence to herself.

Three weeks passed in this way. Natásha had no desire to go out anywhere and wandered from room to room like a shadow, idle and listless; she wept secretly at night and did not go to her mother in the evenings. She blushed continually and was irritable. It seemed to her that everybody knew about her disappointment and was laughing at her and pitying her. Strong as was her inward grief, this wound to her vanity intensified her misery.

Once she came to her mother, tried to say something, and suddenly began to cry. Her tears were those of an offended child who does not know why it is being punished.

The countess began to soothe Natásha, who after first listening to her mother's words, suddenly interrupted her:

"Leave off, Mamma! I don't think, and don't want to think about it! He just came and then left off, left off...."

Her voice trembled, and she again nearly cried, but recovered and went on quietly:

"And I don't at all want to get married. And I am afraid of him; I have now become quite calm, quite calm."

The day after this conversation Natásha put on the old dress which she knew had the peculiar property of conducing to cheerfulness in the mornings, and that day she returned to the old way of life which she had abandoned since the ball. Having finished her morning tea she went to the ballroom, which she particularly liked for its loud resonance, and began singing her solfeggio. When she had finished her first exercise she stood still in the middle of the room and sang a musical phrase that particularly pleased her. She listened joyfully (as though she had not expected it) to the charm of the notes reverberating, filling the whole empty ballroom, and slowly dying away; and all at once she felt cheerful. "What's the good of making so much of it? Things are nice as it is," she said to herself, and she began walking up and down the room, not stepping simply on the resounding parquet but treading with each step from the heel to the toe (she had on a new and favorite pair of shoes) and listening to the regular tap of the heel and creak of the toe as gladly as she had to the sounds of her own voice. Passing a mirror she glanced into it. "There, that's me!" the expression of her face seemed to say as she caught sight of herself. "Well, and very nice too! I need nobody."

A footman wanted to come in to clear away something in the room but she would not let him, and having closed the door behind him continued her walk. That morning she had returned to her favorite mood—love of, and delight in, herself. "How charming that Natásha is!" she said again, speaking as some third, collective, male person. "Pretty, a good voice, young, and in nobody's way if only they leave her in peace." But however much they left her in peace she could not now be at peace, and immediately felt this.

In the hall the porch door opened, and someone asked, "At home?" and then footsteps were heard. Natásha was looking at the mirror, but did not see herself. She listened to the sounds in the hall. When she saw herself, her face was pale. It was *he*. She knew this for certain, though she hardly heard his voice through the closed doors.

Pale and agitated, Natásha ran into the drawing room.

"Mamma! Bolkónski has come!" she said. "Mamma, it is awful, it is unbearable! I don't want... to be tormented? What am I to do?..."

Before the countess could answer, Prince Andrew entered the room with an agitated and serious face. As soon as he saw Natásha his face brightened. He kissed the countess' hand and Natásha's, and sat down beside the sofa.

"It is long since we had the pleasure..." began the countess, but Prince Andrew interrupted her by answering her intended question, obviously in haste to say what he had to.

"I have not been to see you all this time because I have been at my father's. I had to talk over a very important matter with him. I only got back last night," he said glancing at Natásha; "I want to have a talk with you, Countess," he added after a moment's pause.

The countess lowered her eyes, sighing deeply.

"I am at your disposal," she murmured.

Natásha knew that she ought to go away, but was unable to do so: something gripped her throat, and regardless of manners she stared straight at Prince Andrew with wide-open eyes.

"At once? This instant!... No, it can't be!" she thought.

Again he glanced at her, and that glance convinced her that she was not mistaken. Yes, at once, that very instant, her fate would be decided.

"Go, Natásha! I will call you," said the countess in a whisper.

Natásha glanced with frightened imploring eyes at Prince Andrew and at her mother and went out.

"I have come, Countess, to ask for your daughter's hand," said Prince Andrew.

The countess' face flushed hotly, but she said nothing.

"Your offer..." she began at last sedately. He remained silent, looking into her eyes. "Your offer..." (she grew confused) "is agreeable to us, and I accept your offer. I am glad. And my husband... I hope... but it will depend on her...."

"I will speak to her when I have your consent.... Do you give it to me?" said Prince Andrew.

"Yes," replied the countess. She held out her hand to him, and with a mixed feeling of estrangement and tenderness pressed her lips to his forehead as he stooped to kiss her hand. She wished to love him as a son, but felt that to her he was a stranger and a terrifying man. "I am sure my husband will consent," said the countess, "but your father..."

"My father, to whom I have told my plans, has made it an express condition of his consent that the wedding is not to take place for a year. And I wished to tell you of that," said Prince Andrew.

"It is true that Natásha is still young, but—so long as that?..."

"It is unavoidable," said Prince Andrew with a sigh.

"I will send her to you," said the countess, and left the room.

"Lord have mercy upon us!" she repeated while seeking her daughter.

Sónya said that Natásha was in her bedroom. Natásha was sitting on the bed, pale and dry-eyed, and was gazing at the icons and whispering something as she rapidly crossed herself. Seeing her mother she jumped up and flew to her.

"Well, Mamma?... Well?..."

"Go, go to him. He is asking for your hand," said the countess, coldly it seemed to Natásha. "Go... go," said the mother, sadly and reproachfully, with a deep sigh, as her daughter ran away.

Natásha never remembered how she entered the drawing room. When she came in and saw him she paused. "Is it possible that this stranger has now become *everything* to me?" she asked herself, and immediately answered, "Yes, everything! He alone is now dearer to me than everything in the world." Prince Andrew came up to her with downcast eyes.

"I have loved you from the very first moment I saw you. May I hope?"

He looked at her and was struck by the serious impassioned expression of her face. Her face said: "Why ask? Why doubt what you cannot but know? Why speak, when words cannot express what one feels?"

She drew near to him and stopped. He took her hand and kissed it.

"Do you love me?"

"Yes, yes!" Natásha murmured as if in vexation. Then she sighed loudly and, catching her breath more and more quickly, began to sob.

"What is it? What's the matter?"

"Oh, I am so happy!" she replied, smiled through her tears, bent over closer to him, paused for an instant as if asking herself whether she might, and then kissed him.

Prince Andrew held her hands, looked into her eyes, and did not find in his heart his former love for her. Something in him had suddenly changed; there was no longer the former poetic and mystic charm of desire, but there was pity for her feminine and childish weakness, fear at her devotion and trustfulness, and an oppressive yet joyful sense of the duty that now bound him to her forever. The present feeling, though not so bright and poetic as the former, was stronger and more serious.

"Did your mother tell you that it cannot be for a year?" asked Prince Andrew, still looking into her eyes.

"Is it possible that I—the 'chit of a girl,' as everybody called me," thought Natásha—"is it possible that I am now to be the *wife* and the equal of this strange, dear, clever man whom even my father looks up to? Can it be true? Can it be true that there can be no more playing with life, that now I am grown up, that on me now lies a responsibility for my every word and deed? Yes, but what did he ask me?"

"No," she replied, but she had not understood his question.

"Forgive me!" he said. "But you are so young, and I have already been through so much in life. I am afraid for you, you do not yet know yourself."

Natásha listened with concentrated attention, trying but failing to take in the meaning of his words.

"Hard as this year which delays my happiness will be," continued Prince Andrew, "it will give you time to be sure of yourself. I ask you to make me happy in a year, but you are free: our engagement shall remain a secret, and should you find that you do not love me, or should you come to love..." said Prince Andrew with an unnatural smile.

"Why do you say that?" Natásha interrupted him. "You know that from the very day you first came to Otrádnoe I have loved you," she cried, quite convinced that she spoke the truth.

"In a year you will learn to know yourself...."

"A whole year!" Natásha repeated suddenly, only now realizing that the marriage was to be postponed for a year. "But why a year? Why a year?..."

Prince Andrew began to explain to her the reasons for this delay. Natásha did not hear him.

"And can't it be helped?" she asked. Prince Andrew did not reply, but his face expressed the impossibility of altering that decision.

"It's awful! Oh, it's awful! awful!" Natásha suddenly cried, and again burst into sobs. "I shall die, waiting a year: it's impossible, it's awful!" She looked into her lover's face and saw in it a look of commiseration and perplexity.

"No, no! I'll do anything!" she said, suddenly checking her tears. "I am so happy."

The father and mother came into the room and gave the betrothed couple their blessing.

From that day Prince Andrew began to frequent the Rostóvs' as Natásha's affianced lover.

CHAPTER XXIV

No betrothal ceremony took place and Natásha's engagement to Bolkónski was not announced; Prince Andrew insisted on that. He said that as he was responsible for the delay he ought to bear the whole burden of it; that he had given his word and bound himself forever, but that he did not wish to bind Natásha and gave her perfect freedom. If after six months she felt that she did not love him she would have full right to reject him. Naturally neither Natásha nor her parents wished to hear of this, but Prince Andrew was firm. He came every day to the Rostóvs', but did not behave to Natásha as an affianced lover: he did not use the familiar *thou*, but said *you* to her, and kissed only her hand. After their engagement, quite different, intimate, and natural relations sprang up between them. It was as if they had not known each other till now. Both liked to recall how they had regarded each other when as yet they were *nothing* to one another; they felt themselves now quite different beings: then they were artificial, now natural and sincere. At first the family felt some constraint in intercourse with Prince Andrew; he seemed a man from another world, and for a long time Natásha trained the family to get used to him, proudly assuring them all that he only appeared to be different, but was really just like all of them, and that she was not afraid of him and no one else ought to be. After a few days they grew accustomed to him, and without restraint in his presence pursued their usual way of life, in which he took his part. He could talk about rural economy with the count, fashions with the countess and Natásha, and about albums and fancywork with Sónya. Sometimes the household both among themselves and in his presence expressed their wonder at how it had all happened, and at the evident omens there had been of it: Prince

Andrew's coming to Otrádnoe and their coming to Petersburg, and the likeness between Natásha and Prince Andrew which her nurse had noticed on his first visit, and Andrew's encounter with Nicholas in 1805, and many other incidents betokening that it had to be.

In the house that poetic dullness and quiet reigned which always accompanies the presence of a betrothed couple. Often when all sitting together everyone kept silent. Sometimes the others would get up and go away and the couple, left alone, still remained silent. They rarely spoke of their future life. Prince Andrew was afraid and ashamed to speak of it. Natásha shared this as she did all his feelings, which she constantly divined. Once she began questioning him about his son. Prince Andrew blushed, as he often did now—Natásha particularly liked it in him—and said that his son would not live with them.

"Why not?" asked Natásha in a frightened tone.

"I cannot take him away from his grandfather, and besides..."

"How I should have loved him!" said Natásha, immediately guessing his thought; "but I know you wish to avoid any pretext for finding fault with us."

Sometimes the old count would come up, kiss Prince Andrew, and ask his advice about Pétya's education or Nicholas' service. The old countess sighed as she looked at them; Sónya was always getting frightened lest she should be in the way and tried to find excuses for leaving them alone, even when they did not wish it. When Prince Andrew spoke (he could tell a story very well), Natásha listened to him with pride; when she spoke she noticed with fear and joy that he gazed attentively and scrutinizingly at her. She asked herself in perplexity: "What does he look for in me? He is trying to discover something by looking at me! What if what he seeks in me is not there?" Sometimes she fell into one of the mad, merry moods characteristic of her, and then she particularly loved to hear and see how Prince Andrew laughed. He seldom laughed, but when he did he abandoned himself entirely to his laughter, and after such a laugh she always felt nearer to him. Natásha would have been completely happy if the thought of the separation awaiting her and drawing near had not terrified her, just as the mere thought of it made him turn pale and cold.

On the eve of his departure from Petersburg Prince Andrew brought with him Pierre, who had not been to the Rostóvs' once since the ball. Pierre seemed disconcerted and embarrassed. He was talking to the countess, and Natásha sat down beside a little chess table with Sónya, thereby inviting Prince Andrew to come too. He did so.

"You have known Bezúkhov a long time?" he asked. "Do you like him?"

"Yes, he's a dear, but very absurd."

And as usual when speaking of Pierre, she began to tell anecdotes of his absent-mindedness, some of which had even been invented about him.

"Do you know I have entrusted him with our secret? I have known him from childhood. He has a heart of gold. I beg you, Natalie," Prince Andrew said with sudden seriousness—"I am going away and heaven knows what may happen. You may cease to... all right, I know I am not to say that. Only this, then: whatever may happen to you when I am not here..."

"What can happen?"

"Whatever trouble may come," Prince Andrew continued, "I beg you, Mademoiselle Sophie, whatever may happen, to turn to him alone for advice and help! He is a most absent-minded and absurd fellow, but he has a heart of gold."

Neither her father, nor her mother, nor Sónya, nor Prince Andrew himself could have foreseen how the separation from her lover would act on Natásha. Flushed and agitated she went about the house all that day, dry-eyed, occupied with most trivial matters as if not understanding what awaited her. She did not even cry when, on taking leave, he kissed her hand for the last time. "Don't go!" she said in a tone that made him wonder whether he really ought not to stay and which he remembered long afterwards. Nor did she cry when he was gone; but for several days she sat in her room dry-eyed, taking no interest in anything and only saying now and then, "Oh, why did he go away?"

But a fortnight after his departure, to the surprise of those around her, she recovered from her mental sickness just as suddenly and became her old self again, but with a change in her moral physiognomy, as a child gets up after a long illness with a changed expression of face.

CHAPTER XXV

During that year after his son's departure, Prince Nicholas Bolkónski's health and temper became much worse. He grew still more irritable, and it was Princess Mary who generally bore the brunt of his frequent fits of unprovoked anger. He seemed carefully to seek out her tender spots so as to torture her mentally as harshly as possible. Princess Mary had two passions and consequently two joys—her nephew, little Nicholas, and religion—and these were the favorite subjects of the prince's attacks and ridicule. Whatever was spoken of he would bring round to the superstitiousness of old maids, or the petting and spoiling of children. "You want to make him"—little Nicholas—"into an old maid like yourself! A pity! Prince Andrew wants a son and not an old maid," he would say. Or, turning to Mademoiselle Bourienne, he would ask her in Princess Mary's presence how she liked our village priests and icons and would joke about them.

He continually hurt Princess Mary's feelings and tormented her, but it cost her no effort to forgive him. Could he be to blame toward her, or could her father, whom she knew loved her in spite of it all, be unjust? And what is justice? The princess never thought of that proud word "justice." All the complex laws of man centered for her in one clear and simple law—the law of love and self-sacrifice taught us by Him who lovingly suffered for mankind though He Himself was God. What had she to do with the justice or injustice of other people? She had to endure and love, and that she did.

During the winter Prince Andrew had come to Bald Hills and had been gay, gentle, and more affectionate than Princess Mary had known him for a long time past. She felt that something had happened to him, but he said nothing to her about his love. Before he left he had a long talk with his father about something, and Princess Mary noticed that before his departure they were dissatisfied with one another.

Soon after Prince Andrew had gone, Princess Mary wrote to her friend Julie Karágina in Petersburg, whom she had dreamed (as all girls dream) of marrying to her brother, and who was at that time in mourning for her own brother, killed in Turkey.

Sorrow, it seems, is our common lot, my dear, tender friend Julie.

Your loss is so terrible that I can only explain it to myself as a special providence of God who, loving you, wishes to try you and your excellent mother. Oh, my friend! Religion, and religion alone, can—I will not say comfort us—but save us from despair. Religion alone can explain to us what without its help man cannot comprehend: why, for what cause, kind and noble beings able to find happiness in life—not merely harming no one but necessary to the happiness of others—are called away to God, while cruel, useless, harmful persons, or such as are a burden to themselves and to others, are left living. The first death I saw, and one I shall never forget—that of my dear sister-in-law—left that impression on me. Just as you ask destiny why your splendid brother had to die, so I asked why that angel Lise, who not only never wronged anyone, but in whose soul there were never any unkind thoughts, had to die. And what do you think, dear friend? Five years have passed since then, and already I, with my petty understanding, begin to see clearly why she had to die, and in what way that death was but an expression of the infinite goodness of the Creator, whose every action, though generally incomprehensible to us, is but a manifestation of His infinite love for His creatures. Perhaps, I often think, she was too angelically innocent to have the strength to perform all a mother's duties. As a young wife she was irreproachable; perhaps she could not have been so as a mother. As it is, not only has she left us, and particularly Prince Andrew, with the purest regrets and memories, but probably she will *there* receive a place I dare not hope for myself. But not to speak of her alone, that early and terrible death has had the most beneficent influence on me and on my brother in spite of all our grief. Then, at the moment of our loss, these thoughts could not occur to me; I should then have dismissed them with horror, but now they are very clear and certain. I write all this to you, dear friend, only to convince you of the Gospel truth which has become for me a principle of life: not a single hair of our heads will fall without His will. And His will is governed only by infinite love for us, and so whatever befalls us is for our good.

You ask whether we shall spend next winter in Moscow. In spite of my wish to see you, I do not think so and do not want to do so. You will be surprised to hear that the reason for this is Buonaparte! The case is this: my father's health is growing noticeably worse, he cannot stand any contradiction and is becoming irritable. This irritability is, as you know, chiefly directed to political questions. He cannot endure the notion that Buonaparte is negotiating on equal terms with all the sovereigns of Europe and particularly with our own, the grandson of the Great Catherine! As you know, I am quite indifferent to politics, but from my father's remarks and his talks with Michael Ivánovich I know all that goes on in the world and especially about the honors conferred on Buonaparte, who only at Bald Hills in the whole world, it seems, is not accepted as a great man, still less as Emperor of France. And my father cannot stand this. It seems to me that it is chiefly because of his political views that my father is reluctant to speak of going to Moscow; for he foresees the encounters that would result from his way of expressing his views regardless of anybody. All the benefit he might derive from a course of treatment he would lose as a result of the disputes about Buonaparte which would be inevitable. In any case it will be decided very shortly.

Our family life goes on in the old way except for my brother Andrew's absence. He, as I wrote you before, has changed very much of late. After his sorrow he only this year quite recovered his spirits. He has again become as I used to know him when a child: kind, affectionate, with that heart of gold to which I know no equal. He has realized, it seems to me, that life is not over for him. But together with this mental change he has grown physically much weaker. He has become thinner and more nervous. I am anxious about him and glad he is taking this trip abroad which the doctors recommended long ago. I hope it will cure him. You write that in Petersburg he is spoken of as one of the most active, cultivated, and capable of the young men. Forgive my vanity as a relation, but I never doubted it. The good he has done to everybody here, from his peasants up to the gentry, is incalculable. On his arrival in Petersburg he received only his due. I always wonder at the way rumors fly from Petersburg to Moscow, especially such false ones as that you write about—I mean the report of my brother's betrothal to the little Rostóva. I do not think my brother will ever marry again, and certainly not her; and this is why: first, I know that though he rarely speaks about the wife he has lost, the grief of that loss has gone too deep in his heart for him ever to decide to give her a successor and our little angel a stepmother. Secondly because, as far as I know, that girl is not the kind of girl who could please Prince Andrew. I do not think he would choose her for a wife, and frankly I do not wish it. But I am running on too long and am at the end of my second sheet. Good-by, my dear friend. May God keep you in His holy and mighty care. My dear friend, Mademoiselle Bourienne, sends you kisses.

MARY

CHAPTER XXVI

In the middle of the summer Princess Mary received an unexpected letter from Prince Andrew in Switzerland in which he gave her strange and surprising news. He informed her of his engagement to NatáshaRostóva. The whole letter breathed loving rapture for his betrothed and tender and confiding affection for his sister. He wrote that he had never loved as he did now and that only now did he understand and know what life was. He asked his sister to forgive him for not having told her of his resolve when he had last visited Bald Hills, though he had spoken of it to his father. He had not done so for fear Princess Mary should ask her father to give his consent, irritating him and having to bear the brunt of his displeasure without attaining her object. "Besides," he wrote, "the matter was not then so definitely settled as it is now. My father then insisted on a delay of a year and now already *six months*, half of that period, have passed, and my resolution is firmer than ever. If the doctors did not keep me here at the spas I should be back in Russia, but as it is I have to postpone my return for three months. You know me and my relations with Father. I want nothing from him. I have been and always shall be independent; but to go against his will and arouse his anger, now that he may perhaps remain with us such a short time, would destroy half my happiness. I am now writing to him about the same question, and beg you to choose a good moment to hand him the letter and to let me know how he looks at the whole matter and whether there is hope that he may consent to reduce the term by four months."

After long hesitations, doubts, and prayers, Princess Mary gave the letter to her father. The next day the old prince said to her quietly:

"Write and tell your brother to wait till I am dead.... It won't be long—I shall soon set him free."

The princess was about to reply, but her father would not let her speak and, raising his voice more and more, cried:

"Marry, marry, my boy!... A good family!... Clever people, eh? Rich, eh? Yes, a nice stepmother little Nicholas will have! Write and tell him that he may marry tomorrow if he likes. She will be little Nicholas' stepmother and I'll marry Bourienne!... Ha, ha, ha! He mustn't be without a stepmother either! Only one thing, no more women are wanted in my house—let him marry and live by himself. Perhaps you will go and live with him too?" he added, turning to Princess Mary. "Go in heaven's name! Go out into the frost... the frost... the frost!"

After this outburst the prince did not speak any more about the matter. But repressed vexation at his son's poor-spirited behavior found expression in his treatment of his daughter. To his former pretexts for irony a fresh one was now added—allusions to stepmothers and amiabilities to Mademoiselle Bourienne.

"Why shouldn't I marry her?" he asked his daughter. "She'll make a splendid princess!"

And latterly, to her surprise and bewilderment, Princess Mary noticed that her father was really associating more and more with the Frenchwoman. She wrote to Prince Andrew about the reception of his letter, but comforted him with hopes of reconciling their father to the idea.

Little Nicholas and his education, her brother Andrew, and religion were Princess Mary's joys and consolations; but besides that, since everyone must have personal hopes, Princess Mary in the profoundest depths of her heart had a hidden dream and hope that supplied the chief consolation of her life. This comforting dream and hope were given her by *God's folk*—the half-witted and other pilgrims who visited her without the prince's knowledge. The longer she lived, the more experience and observation she had of life, the greater was her wonder at the short-sightedness of men who seek enjoyment and happiness here on earth: toiling, suffering, struggling, and harming one another, to obtain that impossible, visionary, sinful happiness. Prince Andrew had loved his wife, she died, but that was not enough: he wanted to bind his happiness to another woman. Her father objected to this because he wanted a more distinguished and wealthier match for Andrew. And they all struggled and suffered and tormented one another and injured their souls, their eternal souls, for the attainment of benefits which endure but for an instant. Not only do we know this ourselves, but Christ, the Son of God, came down to earth and told us that this life is but for a moment and is a probation; yet we cling to it and think to find happiness in it. "How is it that no one realizes this?" thought Princess Mary. "No one except these despised *God's folk* who, wallet on back, come to me by the back door, afraid of being seen by the prince, not for fear of ill-usage by him but for fear of causing him to sin. To leave family, home, and all the cares of worldly welfare, in order without clinging to anything to wander in hempen rags from place to place under an assumed name, doing no one any harm but praying for all—for those who drive one away as well as for those who protect one: higher than that life and truth there is no life or truth!"

There was one pilgrim, a quiet pockmarked little woman of fifty called Theodosia, who for over thirty years had gone about barefoot and worn heavy chains. Princess Mary was particularly fond of her. Once, when in a room with a lamp dimly lit before the icon Theodosia was talking of her life, the thought that Theodosia alone had found the true path of life suddenly came to Princess Mary with such force that she resolved to become a pilgrim herself. When Theodosia had gone to sleep Princess Mary thought about this for a long time, and at last made up her mind that, strange as it might seem, she must go on a pilgrimage. She disclosed this thought to no one but to her confessor, Father Akínfi, the monk, and he approved of her intention. Under guise of a present for the pilgrims, Princess Mary prepared a pilgrim's complete costume for herself: a coarse smock, bast shoes, a rough coat, and a black kerchief. Often, approaching the chest of drawers containing this secret treasure, Princess Mary paused, uncertain whether the time had not already come to put her project into execution.

Often, listening to the pilgrims' tales, she was so stimulated by their simple speech, mechanical to them but to her so full of deep meaning, that several times she was on the point of abandoning everything and running away from home. In imagination she already pictured herself by Theodosia's side, dressed in coarse rags, walking with a staff, a wallet on her back, along the dusty road, directing her wanderings from one saint's shrine to another, free from envy, earthly love, or desire, and reaching at last the place where there is no more sorrow or sighing, but eternal joy and bliss.

"I shall come to a place and pray there, and before having time to get used to it or getting to love it, I shall go farther. I will go on till my legs fail, and I'll lie down and die somewhere, and shall at last reach that eternal, quiet haven, where there is neither sorrow nor sighing..." thought Princess Mary.

But afterwards, when she saw her father and especially little Koko (Nicholas), her resolve weakened. She wept quietly, and felt that she was a sinner who loved her father and little nephew more than God.